The Call to Serve

By Cece Whittaker

Easton One Productions
Absecon, New Jersey
www.CeceWhittakerStories.com
First Edition, 2017
Second Edition, 2018

ISBN 13: 978-1548536350

ISBN 10: 1548536350

Dedication

For my mother and father,
may all their dreams come true.

Illustration by Joseph R. DiAngelo

Chapter One

Joan took a seat at Helen's dining room table. "Helen, do you think I'll ever get married?" she asked.

Helen looked up suddenly. "What in the world brought that on?"

"Oh I don't know, just, well, Annie and Sylvester, Bernice and Henry. . ."

"They're not engaged! Neither one of them!"

"Well, don't you think it's just a matter of time?"

"I wouldn't give it another thought, Joan. Your friends are all your age or near it. Things may seem urgent right now, but that's just the times—and your ages."

"How old were you when you got married?"

Helen went over to the sink washed the glue from her hands. She had been showing Joan how to make jewelry from little shells. She sat down beside her. "Times were different then, really. I was young, younger than you and Annie."

"Bernice's age?"

"About that," said Helen, nodding. "But it hasn't been an easy road, Honey, no matter how it looks. It's always something and then when you think you're all set, along comes a big war!" Helen looked away and for the first time in a long time, Joan saw her older friend falter. But only for a second. "But he's a tough old cuss. He'll make it through," finished Helen.

"And he's an officer."

"A petty officer, and he's earned that, but there are no guarantees in a war, Joan."

The tea kettle suddenly began to whistle then almost instantly began shrieking for attention.

"The others should be here soon," said Helen. "Would you put the placemats around for me? And you pick out the teacups, all right?"

The china cups hung on hooks nestled deep within a set of walnut shelves in an antique hutch in the far corner of the room. Helen had 16 in all, if you counted the Irish one with the chip. No one ever used it, but it was so pretty Helen could not bring herself to throw it away. She was certain that one day she'd be able to mend it.

Joan picked four blue and white checked cups and saucers. She took matching plates and the white sugar bowl and cream pitcher.

"Oh that looks nice," said Helen as she arrived from the kitchen with a bowl of peaches and a thick glass bottle of cream. The top layer of the cream was darker than the rest, a deep French vanilla tone, and had not yet been mixed in.

"Oooh! Where did you get that?" Joan said.

"Lance, over next to Bernice's. I'm telling you, those farmers are spoiling us. Betty next door got a whole pound of ground beef yesterday when she gave his boys a lift into town. She didn't even know about it until she got home and found it in the

Frigidaire. I guess his wife snuck it in while they were out."

"I know she can use that!" said Joan.

"Any of us could make good use of that!" chuckled Helen.

Just then came a tap on the door, and Bernice let herself in. "Hello!"

"Here's trouble!" called Helen from the dining room. She winked at Joan, who smiled back as they headed together to the door. "Where's Annie?"

"She's parking the car. She wanted to drop me off at your door so I wouldn't mess this up."

"What have you got there?" asked Joan, peering into the container Bernice held tight against her chest.

"It's a honey cake," Bernice said, moving aside as her friend arrived.

"Annie!" Joan sang out as she gave her friend a hug. "Where did you put the old clunker?"

"Somewhere over that way," said Annie in her strong North Jersey accent, "let me in, it's cold!" She was tall and slender with rich, dark wavy locks.

"Isn't it?" said Joan. "I didn't dress for this kind of crazy weather either. Isn't September supposed to be warm?"

"It was 70 this morning," said Annie, "and now it feels like 50. Shew! Brrr!"

"I know!" said Joan. "Give me your coat."

"Helen," Annie said sighing, "this is really a pleasure. Thank you so much!"

Helen waved her off. "It's just as much a treat for me," she said.

"Well," said Annie, "speaking of treats. . ."

All three of the others perked up. Annie casually put her pocketbook down on a table and started to take off her coat. She sure knew how to get attention.

"Well?" said Joan.

"Well what?" said Annie, snickering.

"Okay, out with it!" Bernice said reaching for Annie's pocketbook. "What ya got in there?"

Annie swiped it away just before she could get a grip on it. Everyone laughed at the scuffle that followed.

"All right, all right!" shouted Annie. "Give a girl a chance." She opened her pocketbook, "here!" She handed Bernice four one-pound Hershey Bars.

Bernice's eyes grew wide, and her mouth shot open. She looked at Helen and Joan, then back at the candy bars, then at Annie. "Where'd you get them? Sylvester! Sylvester got them for you!"

Annie laughed. "No," she said, "believe it or not, it wasn't Sylvester this time. I was just getting ready to close the shop and this man comes in and says he needs Our Lady of Grace—it doesn't matter what; statue, holy card, rosary, whatever I have with Our Lady of Grace. I told him take your pick and he took that statue—you know the one?" she looked at Joan.

"Yes, the one on top shelf there?"

"Yes! The big giant one with the pink roses at her feet. And I said you know that's $28 and he says 'I don't care, Miss, I will take it.' And so I packed it all up nice for him, and off he starts to go. Then he says, 'Hey, wait a minute, I'll be right back!' And he comes back and hands me five candy bars! I about fell down right then and there. 'I sell these,' he says, 'and it's nothing to me, but I want you to have these.' I said, 'Sir, you know, I only helped you find—' and he cuts me off, says he's leaving them, and off he goes," Annie's eyes grew wide, "whistling Ave Maria!"

Everyone laughed, except Bernice.

"What's the matter with you?" asked Joan, wiping her eyes.

"*Five,* huh?" said Bernice.

"What?" said Helen.

Annie started to giggle again. "Said five, did you?" Bernice repeated.

Joan and Helen looked at Annie.

"Hey—I saved you each one!" she laughed, collapsing onto a chair.

"You *ate* a whole one?" Bernice demanded.

"I did, I admit it," Annie said, trying, but then unable to sustain seriousness.

"You better watch it, Bernice," Joan teased, "she might eat yours, too!"

Bernice grabbed one and quickly put it in her craft bag. "Oh no you don't!"

"Hey, I didn't even offer you one yet," Annie said.

Joan and Helen exchanged glances with Annie. "Kids," said Helen.

Annie fanned out the remaining three and Joan and Helen each took one, tucking it securely away for later. Such a special treat would be enjoyed in bits and pieces and throughout the coming week or two, ever so carefully budgeted.

After tea, Helen disappeared up the stairs.

Joan watched her, and Annie nudged her on the elbow. "She's a wonderful woman, isn't she?"

Joan nodded. She felt a lump in her throat. She looked at Annie with tears in her eyes.

"Harry will be fine, Joanie," Annie said, patting her friend on the shoulder. "He's strong, a survivor. Made it through the last one okay, didn't he?"

Joan sighed and nodded again.

Suddenly Bernice presented herself in the kitchen doorway, standing as tall as her five-foot-two inches could manage. "Do you expect me to do all the work while you lazy girls sit around and gab?"

"*Do you expect me to do all the work?*" Joan mimicked playfully, grabbing the dishtowel from her. "What if I said 'yes'?"

As they disappeared noisily into the kitchen, Helen returned carrying a stack of craft boxes that reached as high as her eyes. "My stars," she said. "All that fuss over four plates and four forks." But she knew "her" girls, and said it with a twinkle in her eye.

"Oh Helen! Let me help you," said Annie taking some of the boxes. "Oh my gosh! Look at these beautiful things! What are they?"

"Didn't Joan tell you?"

"Well, she did, but not, oh my gosh," Annie interrupted herself, putting down the stack and opening up one box. "Look at these pearls!"

"They're just glass, Honey," Helen chuckled.

"They sure look real," Annie said, unfastening the top and running her fingers through the section of the box that held them. "They're so smooth!"

"See those little holes in them?" Helen said taking hold of one and putting it up near the light.

"Mm hmm."

"That's how you string them, with wire or with heavy thread and use them to make your jewelry. They're sure to go over at the bazaar with so little costume jewelry in the shops these days." She shook out a table cover and laid it over top of her linens.

Joan and Bernice joined them.

"Grab a chair, everyone," Helen said, spreading out the boxes on the table cover. "I made a few samples earlier, just to give you an idea of what you can make. We'll all give it a try, okay?"

As the four ladies delved into the project, a gentle September sun slowly settled on the horizon. A block and a half away, the bells of St. Benedict's tolled 3:00, the signal for devotees to begin the recitation of the Divine Mercy Chaplet. The radiant sun sent rays through the stained-glass windows, silhouetting those inside as gentle, kneeling shadows within the holy refuge.

Wrinkled, grey-haired, soulfully impassioned, Father Joseph Bertrand stood at the entryway just inside the church. He smiled, grateful for the attendance. St. Benedict's had seen much slower times over its 79 years. In fact, some days during the later '20s, he had been the singular participant in 3:00 prayers. On those days, Father Bertrand carried on straight through, saying prayers alone for the sake of his city and the world as it was. In 1939, a dear friend and priest from Poland, Father Alphonse Kuchesky, had brought him the news of a Blessed Faustina and her messages from God by way of the Divine Mercy Prayer.

Father Bertrand, sensing that the prayer was extremely important, particularly at that time of the world, immediately committed it to memory, as well as the subsequent Chaplet, designed to fall in line with the beads of the rosary. Three o'clock, ironically, turned out to be the designated hour for the holy chaplet to be prayed and the new devotee of Poland's Faustina immediately instituted the Divine Mercy Chaplet as the 3:00 prayer. The word of the miraculous Chaplet spread rapidly throughout Catholic communities across the country. As more and more participated in it, the pastor instituted a 3:00 bell ringing to complement the 6:00 for the Angelus.

Then, just before Christmas of 1939, Father Kuchesky had disappeared in Poland, along with masses of other Catholics and Jews in the aftermath of the September 1st German invasion. It was two years later, on the ugly day in December of 1941, after the Japanese Pearl Harbor air raid massacre, and the more than 2400 American dead, St. Benedict's daily prayer hours rapidly filled to capacity. From that point forward, through the bombings of London, the bombings of Germany, the battles at Midway, Guadalcanal, and then the invasion of North Africa where so many Americans were in jeopardy, Father Bertrand's parishioners seemed to have completely regained consciousness of the deeper meaning of life.

Father Bertrand was happy for the attendance, and because of it, he held out hope for the success of the United States. He felt very little fear, although there were times when his optimism failed him as he thought of Father Kuchesky, and the fates of the others. He had written to the Diocese of Krakow but they, too, had completely lost touch with the priest. It was clear that they had concluded the worst.

When the recitation of the Chaplet was over, some parishioners approached the shining rack of lit candles in search of unlit ones to light with their special prayers and requests of God and the saints. After lighting a candle, the faithful would kneel on the padded kneeler in front of the statue of the Blessed Mother, and make his or her request. Others lingered within the church, content to be in solitary prayer.

Father Bertrand wished the last departing parishioners a pleasant afternoon and then entered the sacristy to prepare for the vesper service later that afternoon.

Chatting happily as they descended the front steps of the church were two elderly ladies, each close to eighty years old, and in remarkably good shape.

"Bernice is working on it today," said Clara, a taller, slightly bow-legged woman. "She said this year, she's not baking, but *making*!" Clara's eyes lit up with mischief. "Well, if her making is as good as her baking, we'd best steer clear!"

"Oh Clara!" laughed Rose. "You say the funniest things."

"No meanness intended, don't you know," said Clara. "She is a dear grandchild, but oh how I wish her mother would teach her to cook!"

"Well, the way I understand it, Clara," Rose said, "she has done her best under the circumstances." She pursed her lips, following Clara's every move to determine her answer.

But Clara just raised her eyebrows and looked straight ahead. "It's not nice to gossip, you know."

Rose scowled and shook her head.

The two ladies proceeded down Walnut Street, turned right, and stopped one block later on 23rd at Clara's little cottage. "Do come in for coffee, Rose," said Clara.

"Don't mind if I do," said Rose.

Chapter Two

"Oh gosh," Annie said looking at the clock, "fifteen minutes 'til vespers. You're going, aren't you?" she asked Joan.

"Yes, I am," said Joan. "Helen, we can come back and clean up afterwards. If that's okay."

"It'll have to be," said Helen, "because I'm going, too!"

Bernice put her hands on her hips. "Well what am I supposed to do? I'm not going to church. I have to. . . help my mom."

"Come on when we go," Helen said. "We'll all walk down together."

On the table as they departed sat the beginnings of one tiny hat, made of pink, white, and red shells, waiting expectantly in Annie's place. Where Helen sat, a completed yellow and white rose pin sat drying, and a small collection of tiny yellow, white, and dark green shells. Her yellow and white rose was fitted with 3 dark green shells to form the leaves, and a little round backing held it all together. Glued to the opposite side of the little circle with Duco's Cement was a metal pin and twist clasp fastener. In front of Joan's place was a tiny boot made up of rose and brown shells, with flowers at the top of it in blue and white. Where Bernice had sat was a collection of shells, many shapes, sizes, and colors, and three glued together but not actually forming anything recognizable.

"All right," Bernice said.

"Your rose is beautiful, Helen," Annie said. "You should give lessons."

"Oh, I think you're getting the hang of it!" Helen came back. "I never would have thought to make a little fashion hat!"

"Not me either, Annie," said Joan. "I only thought of the boot because of your hat. It's adorable!"

Bernice scowled. "How do you like my big clump of *nothing*?" she demanded.

As Helen held the door open for them, she gave Bernice a warm smile. "It's your first try, Honey, and you're a little younger. Remember, not everyone has a knack for shell craft. You might be better at one of the other things."

"Like what?"

"What about needlework?" said Joan. "Crocheting is fun, and knitting, or embroidery."

"I don't know," said Bernice as they walked down the lane. "I just don't have the coordination for that kind of stuff."

"I bet if you tried you could," said Annie. "Some of that stuff is just natural to people, and others, well they gotta try a little more."

"Not you guys!" said Bernice. "I don't know, I just think I'm more, well, I don't know. I just don't really have any talent."

"Everybody's got talent," said Joan.

"You said it!" said Helen. "We'll figure it out."

"Yeah, stick with us, kid," said Annie, in her best Humphrey Bogart.

"Okay, but I can tell you what one of your talents is *not*," said Bernice.

At the crossroads of 23rd and Walnut, they parted. Bernice lived down 23rd, where her parents had settled in a home right next to where her father grew up. Bernice waved as she turned down her street. "I'll see you guys later!"

"Say hello to your mom for me," said Helen. "I hope she's feeling better."
Annie and Joan exchanged glances. They all walked in silence for a while. The bells began to ring just as they entered the church.

"Let's sit up front," said Annie.

Joan made a face, but went along. Helen stifled a chuckle.

"I just don't like feeling like I'm on stage," Joan whispered.

The prayer service was warm and peaceful. At the end, just as they were leaving, a newspaper boy at the corner called an "Extra." People on their way home from work had stopped their cars to grab a copy. Ladies in aprons in the midst of making dinner were rushing down their walks, some with dishtowels still in hand, joining nearly everyone exiting from St. Benedict's to reach the newsboy.

Through the crowd, Helen managed to slink in close, hand the boy a dime, and snatch a copy before the he was sold out. She had a knack that way. But she also had a reason. The Extra was most certainly about the War, as they all were those days.

"What's it say?" Joan asked urgently. "You'd think the kid could say more than 'Extra, Extra!'"

"He's so young yet, Joanie," said Annie, looking over Joan's head at the paper.

Helen shook her head and handed it to Joan. "The Germans took over Rome," she said very quietly.

"No," said Annie. "It can't be. Italy surrendered, they put Mussolini in jail! He's in jail!"

"Not anymore he isn't," said Helen. "The Germans let him out today. And put him back in charge."

The girls stood there in a huddle, reading together, as did other little groups dotting the intersection and side streets. Then slowly the sidewalks cleared, the silence almost as poignant as the rush to get the news.

"Well, let's not let it get us down, girls," said Helen as they walked along. "We've got lots of things to do yet, and the boys will need our help more than ever now."

"You think they'll keep calling them up?" Annie asked nobody in particular.

"Oh, well, yes. . ." said Helen. "I don't see how they couldn't—well, you know, with all this going on. . ." Her voice trailed off as they moved along. Joan elbowed her. She nodded.

"Sylvester's almost done his second year," Annie said, almost conversationally, as if she'd just introduced him to the girls.

"They'll let him finish college, Annie," Joan said. "They're mostly calling up the ones you know, that. . ."

Annie put an arm around her friend. "They're mostly calling up ones that don't have families," she said. "They can't be worrying about whether or not a fellow's trying to make it through college. Not at a time like this."

They were silent again for a bit. Then Joan spoke hesitantly. "Do you even. . .have an *idea*, Helen, where Ralph might be?"

"All I know is they didn't need them in Africa anymore, so he probably went to Europe. That's all I know. In some ways," she said thoughtfully, "it's better, I guess. I can still, you know, imagine that he's maybe on school crossing duty in Canada."

"Or fitness training at the Washington Zoo."

"Oh no, not Washington, maybe Cleveland."

"Or," Annie chimed in, "standing guard at the Arlington Cemetery."

"No, that's Marine's," Joan said. "Harry's Navy."

"Well then the Navy cemetery."

"What Navy cemetery?" said Joan. "There's no Navy cemetery."

"Oh they got lots of 'em!" Annie said. "Everbody's gotta be buried—" She stopped suddenly. The game had suddenly taken a wrong turn. Joan and Annie exchanged glances.

"Oh don't worry!" Helen laughed out loud. "Nobody's getting buried today anyway! Now we're here. Let's finish and clean up. I know you girls need to get back."

It was very dark at 23ʰ and Arden as Annie and Joan turned up the drive to number 7401.

"I'm telling you, Annie, we've got to put up some lights," Joan said. "It's too dark back here."

"I know it. That's what Sylvester says." Annie turned the key and stepped inside. "I'll start the oven and put in the casserole."

"Let me just put these little things away," Joan said, indicating the small box that held their two shell creations. "Mine needs to dry a bit more and I don't want to forget where I put it!"

"Okay, would you mind setting mine on something to dry, too? I might have started before you but I put a ton of glue on there!"

"Yep, and don't forget to telephone your mom."

"I will. So many things for a working girl to do."

Joan carried the box carefully, took off the lid, and checked the two pieces of jewelry that she and Annie had created; the fashion hat, and the boot holding flowers. "I really can't find fault with either one of these," she said to herself nodding. "We did a pretty good job."

"Poor Bernice," Joan said, joining Annie in the kitchen. "Would you like something hot to drink?"

"Mmhm. Thanks. Why poor Bernice?"

"Well I don't think she says it but I think she feels pretty bad about not being, you know, artistic or. . ."

"Coordinated?" laughed Annie. "No, she's fine. She's a tough cookie, that Bernice."

"I wonder though. She's always saying how she's shorter, and she's not this and not that."

"She's adorable and she knows it. Don't worry about Bernice. It's *you* I'm worried about."

"Me?"

"Yes, you. Helen mentioned you're all stirred up again about. . ."
They exchanged glances.

"Men," they said simultaneously and both broke into laughter.

"You want sugar in this, Annie?"

"Do we *have* sugar?"

"Looks like just about a half a cup, but plenty for tea if we're not going to be baking anything until Monday."

"Okay, sounds great! Thanks."

They sat down together at the round kitchen table alongside a window facing the back of their little rented house. The floor was of wide dark boards, stained and varnished a deep walnut, and covered in large part by a thick oval rug. "It's nice to be home," Joan said.

"It is that," said Annie. "Who would ever think I'd have found such a nice spot to live, and during these times, too?"

Joan smiled. "I'm glad you did!" she said.

"Do you miss your mom, Joan?" Annie asked sincerely.

"Oh yeah, sometimes, a lot I guess," said Joan deep in thought. She got up and went to the window of the little living room beside the kitchen, parted the thick curtains slightly and looked out.

"It's a calm night tonight," said Annie. "She could probably hear you."

Joan nodded. She opened the window and called out, "Hey mom!"

Across the driveway of the house next door, a crack of light shone as a woman appeared at the window above. She wore a housecoat of red and brown check, and her hair, styled in the front, was mostly covered by a large blue scarf. "Hi Honey! Home safe and sound?"

Annie joined Joan at the window.

"Hi Annie! Good to see you two are doing all right." She turned to her husband who was sitting beside the window. "They're back home and looking good."

"Hello there," he stood and called out the window. "Makin' the grade?"

The girls laughed. It was the same thing he always said. "Yep!" laughed Annie. "I got a B+ today. Joan got an A."

"All right then," Joan's mother said. "We'll see you for breakfast on Sunday after the 10:00."

"Okay," Joan said, "but you'll probably see us on the way to Mass, too!"

The girls closed the window to the sound of Mrs. Foster's light and merry laugh.

"We've got about 20 more minutes on that casserole," Annie said. "Do you want to play cards?"

"Sure." Joan got out the deck of cards from a drawer in the kitchen table. "Rummy?"

"Sounds good."

As Joan dealt the cards, Annie said, "We've got to be the best Gin Rummy players in the state of New Jersey.

"I wouldn't be surprised, Annie."

"Speaking of the State of New Jersey," Annie said and then paused, waiting for Joan to look up, which she eventually did.

"What?"

"Well, Leonard over at St. Benedict's, tall guy, with the shaggy hair—"

"Oh Annie! I really don't think he's my type!"

Annie giggled. "I definitely agree… considering he's *married!*" she paused. "Now, as I was saying, Leonard, who is married, told me about a trip they're offering. I cannot go, and really wouldn't want to anyway because the idea is you meet someone nice and I already know someone nice. But I thought you and my friend Margaret might want to be roommates. It's on the weekend so you wouldn't miss work or anything."

Joan was intrigued. "What kind of a trip? Where?"

"It's just into the city, but they've got a block of hotel rooms for all the guests, and you stay two to a room. They have a few activities planned and there are going to be buses from as far away as Washington, D.C."

"Wow that does sound like a big deal. How many people?"

"Leonard said it's like 48 or 50 total, and just about equal numbers of guys and gals."

Joan sat nodding.

"It won't cost you anything since I'm giving you my place, but you should take some spending money."

"Where are they going to find men at a time like this?"

"That's what I wanted to know. But apparently there's a Catholic club for the enlistees. If they're not called up to report in the next little while, they watch the bulletin board for classes in things and social events. I think some of them will be coming."

Joan sat thinking. "Gosh Annie, it sounds like a really nice time!"

"You take your green chiffon, okay? You look so great in that!"

"Thanks, and I will. I don't think I've got anything else. . ."

"Well I'll lend you my light blue. I know I'm tall, but you can pull it off. It will still look great. We'll check and see, how about that? If not, we'll just give it a little hem."

Joan was suddenly full of hope and promise. She grabbed her friend's hand and then got up to give her a big hug. "You are the best friend a girl could have Annie diRosa!"

Suddenly the phone rang. "Oh, that's Mom," said Annie. "I'm gonna get it!"

At 6:00 am next morning, the rain was falling in torrents. "Buckets," Joan's mother would say. It was dark and the street lights were still on. As Joan put on her raincoat, she remembered her conversation with Annie from the night before about the trip into Atlantic City. For some reason, it gave her a kind of fresh and unfamiliar thrill to think of being on her own, well, with Margaret, but mostly on her own in a strange town. Actually, it wasn't a strange town at all. Hmm, she thought. What in the world has gotten into me?

She walked to the corner, the rain so far, not leaking through. She thought of Annie, still snug in bed until 8:00. Her friend had a great job, Joan thought, working at the gift shop like that, and the fact that it had been her uncle's and that he had simply offered it to her was amazing. That sort of thing did not happen often. But as it happened, when he'd enlisted, he'd decided he would take a different path in his life. He would not be able to manage the daily maintenance and demands of running a religious gift shop.

Annie had lived at home then, closer to the city. But she had no car, nor had her family a car, and neither the buses nor the streetcars ran where she needed to be. Besides, Annie at 20 years old, had wanted to get out of her family home, stuffed full of siblings and extended family, and find her way in the world, or at least in southern New Jersey.

It happened that Joan had wanted the same thing. Having met at St. Ann's Catholic High School, they'd stayed in touch. When Joan's great grandmother had died many years before, she had bequeathed her home, which was right beside Joan's house, to Joan's father. For a while they had rented out the home to folks waiting for their homes to be built in neighboring towns, but ten years before, just about all building stopped, as there was not much money coming or going except in the food industries.

Annie's father and uncle owned a dairy farm, and Annie's aunt and two older cousins ran a restaurant in the city. It was actually Joan who mustered the courage to ask her father if she and Annie could live in the house next door.

"We'd take good care of it, Dad, and maybe Annie could give some, and I could pay from my job."

To her surprise, her parents did not put up much of a fight. And Annie's parents, delighted to have such an easy solution, offered to provide some of the rare and precious commodities as well as fresh bread, cookies and even butter from the restaurant every week. As it had turned out, the dairy truck stopped off at Joan's parents' house every Monday with a pound of sugar, breads of all kinds, and usually a nice lasagna or stuffed shells, as well as a ricotta cheesecake or cannoli or both and the butter. Joan's mother always dropped off a share to the girls at 7401.

Joan was joined by some of the regulars as she stood waiting. Together the working women shivered under their umbrellas or clustered under the small shielded area of the bus stop. Finally, the old bus toddled down the lumpy road, gears cranking it down to a stop. A nearly hairless driver opened the door and watched for the proper fares from the fingers of each passenger being released into the slot leading to the long, thin fare receptacle.

Joan found a seat near the front and watched as Abbotsville slowly slipped and bounced out of view for the morning.

Annie listened to the music in her dream. Wasn't that, yes, it was Bach. His concerti, bright and cheerful, sounded like a little flock of birds on a spring morning. It was a bright morning, or was it? She opened her eyes and, gosh, it was dark. Was that Bach? And it was really dark? How could that be?

She rolled over and thought for a minute. Then she heard the rain. Aha. Suddenly Bach didn't sound so much like a concerto but more like a sustained note on the piccolo. Annie struggled to rise and relieve the room of the high-pitched tone, growing more and more annoying by the second. Just as she was on her feet, the alarm clock exhausted itself and sat gasping on her bureau, or so it seemed to Annie.

She had one thought on her mind: Coffee. Oh, it was bleak! Dark and rainy, and no coffee percolating.

Annie had been raised to persevere however, and to the bathroom she proudly stumbled. Once the iced cold water was on her face and she'd caught her breath, she felt pieces of reality start to focus.

Passing Joan's neat, tidy bedroom, all made up and straightened, as she progressed toward the

kitchen, her loosely belted robe flowing out to the
sides, Annie felt for the hundredth time, so very sorry
for her dear roommate who had such a tough life.
How, she thought, does one get up and out by 6:00
am? But in her heart of hearts she knew it to be not
only possible but a constant reality.

The mornings that her father had slept beyond
3:30 a.m. were few and far between. And the bang
bang bang on the front door, sending all the
neighborhood dogs into an explosion of objections
was a daily routine Annie had endeavored to store
away in some distant compartment of her brain,
never to be revisited.

"Okay, Sal!" her Uncle Fabrizzio would call out.
"Ready when you are!"

And clunk clunk clunk down the long steps of the
Newark row home her father would go, holding in
one hand his notebook containing whatever ideas he
had written down for that day. In the other hand, he
carried a bag with lunch in it for him and Fabrizzio.
"On the way!" he would cheerfully call out, and they
would start talking immediately as they hurried to
the truck sitting waiting in the street.

Annie had been awakened every time. And when
she turned 16 and the family bought a farm in South
Jersey, and lived right in Atlantic City, the former
schedule prevailed. While it was somewhat helpful
on the days that she attended early Mass at St. Nick's,
moving out to Joan's parents' rental house in
Abbotsville had been a dream come true. She had
never slept so well in her life. Yet some days, like

Joan, she missed the warm bosom of the family home. And while she and Joan were both very good and thrifty cooks, she missed the daily smell of garlic and *popo* or *scungili*, or just plain old *calamari*. Sometimes.

It had been a blessing in another, deeper way that Annie had moved to the "country" (all of 4 miles from the city). Her selling and bookkeeping skills being excellent, and her naturally buoyant personality made her a perfect candidate for the role of manager of the gift shop. And it was into that gift shop one afternoon that a tall, serious-looking man had wandered.

"Excuse me ma'am," he said to Annie, whose back was turned. "Do you sell statues of —

Just then Annie had turned. Her smile paralyzed him.

"Oh, I mean *Miss*," he corrected rapidly.

"Hmm?" Annie had responded, quick on her feet as ever, "statues of Oh I mean Miss. . . I've never heard of him — or is it a her?"

The young man stepped back, not sure how to answer, his dark eyes puzzling over whether this was a true idiot or actually a very witty, as well as beautiful, woman.

Annie gave it away when she giggled and offered her hand. "Ann diRosa," she said. "And please forgive my idiotic sense of humor."

"Oh!" the man said, "I was just thinking that!"

Then, horrified at what he had said, he gasped. Annie gasped. And the two of them stood stock still

for exactly two seconds—then both burst out
laughing.

"I really didn't mean what I said," he said, "And
by the way, Sylvester Bapini."

"Nice to know you," Annie said. "I should hope
not!"

It had taken exactly that long for the two of them
to fall in love.

Sylvester was an intelligent mathematician, living
on the campus of Rutgers College in New Brunswick,
with the intent of earning a degree in either
mathematics or engineering. He had decided on a
whim to go down to Atlantic City and see what the
city looked like in Spring.

Like most all young men, he had registered for the
draft. He had no objection whatsoever to serving his
country, but neither did he have a deep fervor for it.
So as the War went on, he continued with college the
best he could, knowing that at some point during his
studies, he was likely to be called to serve.

Annie began to understand the feeling that her
cousin Dolores had tried to describe to her, "the
waiting," and how it made one nervous nearly to the
point of giddiness if one thought about it much.
When she talked about it to Joan, Annie got the true
sense that Joan, with her natural compassion,
understood every word she said. It was comforting to
Annie, and brought the two girls closer. And
although Annie wanted Joan to find a man with all
her heart, she also did not want her sensitive friend

to have to deal with the kind of painful anticipation she now felt over Sylvester and the War.

"We can only hope for the best," Helen had said when she'd confided in her. "Joan may surprise us and be the strongest of all. You never know what will happen until you're in a situation yourself. Bernice could turn out to be stronger still."

Bernice, dating her steady boyfriend Henry for over a year, seemed less aware of the danger, Annie thought. She seemed to be simply going along as usual, blissfully unaware that at any moment, her boyfriend, the love of her life, could be called up, inducted, and sent packing off to a foreign war.

That morning, as Annie sat sipping coffee and looking at *Look Magazine*, thoughts of Bernice crept into her defogging mind. Bernice was an enigma. On the one hand, she was a funny, lightweight character who couldn't do many of the artsy things or womanly kitcheny things that she and Joan fell into naturally. She seemed almost like a tomboy. Yet on the other hand, she was careful not to be overly open with her friends. She was a little secretive, Annie decided.

Wishing not to be gossipy but having trouble fighting her creative urges, Annie imagined that maybe Bernice was a secret agent, leading a double life. She played the young clumsy single gal, but in real life, she owned a gun and a pair of binoculars. Annie started to giggle. She went on. And she's got codes, all kinds of secret codes, and oaths. When she sees Joan, Helen, and her, Annie decided, she is to report back on the men in their lives and what they are doing, where they've been sent. And then she generates that message in one of her secret codes. She can't use the telephone because there are people listening—so she uses. . .she sends messages in stitching—no that won't work, Annie giggled. She can't sew. . .

Before she could get much further, she heard a sudden hard knock on the front door.

Annie stood up quickly, pulled her robe tight and heading for the front door, peered between the curtains. What in the world? At 9:00 in the morning? Speak of the devil!

Annie opened the door. "Mrs. St. John, come in out of that rain!" she said.

Bernice's mother, Pauline St. John, a hefty but well-balanced woman, quickly left the rain behind and closed the door. "I'm sorry to bother you so early," she said, her Scottish brogue acting up fiercely. "But I was wondering if she, if Bernice that is, told you where she was going."

Annie stared at Mrs. St. John for a few seconds, waiting for her to finish her question. When it occurred to her that there wasn't any more to come, she opened her mouth to give an answer, and then realized she didn't have one. "Um. . .where. . ."

Mrs. St. John mistook her slowness. "Okay, I know how young girls are, don't want you to be telling tales on each other. But I'm worried. I've talked to Henry and—"

"No, no," Annie cut in, "I, let me—I'm a little slow in the morning—"

"Morning! It's past 9:00!" exclaimed the round little woman.

"Yes, you're right of course. I guess, what I'm trying to say is that this is the first I've heard of Bernice going anywhere. The very first. Honestly, Mrs. St. John. I haven't heard from her and she didn't say anything yesterday."

"Then you saw her yesterday?"

"Yes, at Helen's, with Joan. She went home when we went to Vespers."

"So she was with you 'til 6:00 then? Hmm."

"What's this about Henry?" Annie asked cautiously.

"Oh, when she left me that note, he was the first one I thought of—they're getting married, I thought. But I was wrong, not only is he here, but he has no idea what she's talking about in the note, so he says, anyway."

Annie began to take control of the situation. "Mrs. St. John," she said, "come on in and have some tea. My uncle dropped off a fresh ricotta cake, and a nice slice of it will go very well, and you can tell me the story from the beginning."

Mrs. St. John followed her into the kitchen and took a seat. "Haven't you got any coffee?"

Annie stood with her back to her, grimacing, looking for a clean cup. "So she left you a note. . . "

"Ah, yes, from the beginning. Last night, after I got in from my errands, only about half past 6, I

called to her room and she wasn't there. I figured she
was with you girls. I thought she'd had something
planned for the bazaar crafting."

"Yes, we did, and she was with us for that."

"Okay, so that's all fine and well. But half hour
later, I checked her room and she wasn't there. Her
closet door was open and I noticed her blue and
white pinafore dress missing. She didn't wear that
yesterday, did she?"

"No," Annie said, shaking her head. She brought
over the cup and a plate as the percolator heated on
the stove. "She was wearing her grey and blue
checked jumper with the pretty yellow blouse with
the bowed sleeves."

"Right. That's how I remembered it. But the dress
was gone! And not in the laundry, mind you. And
that jumper's gone too, by the way. Then I saw her
little day case was gone. Immediately I began to
think!" Mrs. St. John grew dramatic.

Annie had the sudden expectation that she was
watching Sherlock Holmes's grandmother at work.
She battled to keep her face straight and respectful.
She lost and turned back to the stove for cover.

"It must have to do with that Henry!" Mrs. St.
John went on. "They've been keeping company for a
long time, and it's reasonable they'll marry soon.
Perhaps they've decided to go and tie the knot secret
like!"

"Oh Mrs. St. John, I don't think so!" Annie said.
"Bernice isn't that kind of a girl. She would want. . ."

Annie stopped, not sure how to go on. "Well, I know she's not that kind," she finished.

"You're so right!" Mrs. St. John snapped. "She's not that kind of a girl at all. If she'd gone off with Henry, he wouldn't be here in Abbotsville, would he? No. And it was then," she said pointing her finger in the air, "that I found the note."

"Note?"

The percolator began to bubble and Annie quickly lifted it before it could throttle up. She filled Mrs. St. John's cup.

"Yes, she'd left me a note!"

"Well, does it say where she went?"

"Yes, it does."

Annie stared at Mrs. St. John, perplexed. "Well, why are you asking me—"

"Because I don't believe it."

"Don't believe that I don't know, or don't believe what the note says?"

Mrs. St. John stirred her coffee. "No cake?"

"Oh!" Annie jumped back up. "I'm sorry!" She flopped a generous slice onto her guest's plate. She put the cake cover back on and quickly sat back down.

Mrs. St. John tore ferociously into the cake.

You'd think it was her last meal, Annie thought. At least the stress doesn't seem to have affected her appetite.

"I feel better now."

"Oh I'm glad," Annie said. "Maybe you just needed a little pick me up."

"Yes, I think you could be right," Mrs. St. John said, smiling. She stood up and reached for her pocketbook. "Thank you, dear. It's nice to know my Bernice has such nice friends. Do give her a call when she gets back home."

Annie stood up again and struggled to keep up with Mrs. St. John as she bee-lined for the door, grabbing her umbrella. "But, Mrs. St. John, you haven't said where Bernice. . . went. . ."

"Oh," said Mrs. St. John, halfway down the walk to the street, "she went to visit her aunt in Philadelphia. Bye bye now, the rain and all." And then she crossed the street, turned right, and disappeared around the corner."

Annie stood watching, bewildered, and giving serious thought to the theory that it had all been some mad plan to get a piece of the beloved diRosa Ricotta Cheesecake. After all, it was well-known in the neighborhood that the diRosa bakery truck stopped next door every Monday.

Annie cleared the dishes, washed them up quickly, and got dressed for work. Later, outside, under her umbrella as the rain continued to fall, she wondered if maybe Joan's life *was* any harder than hers.

Chapter Three

Helen opened the mail and chuckled. It wasn't a Ralph Letter Day, she thought, remembering her little play on words for the sake of the nervous girls, but she did get mail from a soldier. From two soldiers, actually. On the envelope was neatly typed: Your Soldier Penfriends.

Putting the letter down, Helen decided to wait until she saw Joan. They could open them together. It might cheer her up. She'd no sooner done that than Bernice tapped on the door.

"Come in, come in!" said Helen, "Oh! Look at that rain!"

"Hi. I can't believe it's still coming down. It's been like this since early this morning."

"You were up early?" asked Helen with a twinkle. "I didn't see you at Mass."

"Well I was there," said Bernice mischievously, "just not at St. Benedict's."

Helen's eyebrows rose. "Oh really? Where did you go today?"

"I was. . . in my aunt's neck of the words," she said, "in Philadelphia."

"Oh, isn't that nice," said Helen. "I didn't know you had an aunt there."

"I have five all together," Bernice said, "and they all live pretty close, or by train, you know. It's Aunt

Kate in Philadelphia. She has a nice house and a really pretty garden. Too bad it's fading now with fall and all. And all this rain."

"You're right about that!" agreed Helen. "Come on in. I was just about to make some dough, but how about a cup of cocoa instead? Does your aunt have any mums?"

"She's my mother's sister," said Bernice, taking a seat. "What kind of dough are you making?"

Helen looked puzzled for a moment, but let it go. "I saw a recipe for a rye bread made with molasses. I've still got plenty of molasses," Helen said laughing. "Remember the fair last year, the prize was a two-gallon jug of molasses? I'm sure glad you girls were there to help me get it home!"

Bernice giggled. "I still can't believe you can drive a tractor, Helen. Golly." Her voice quivered ever so subtly on that last word. Then she grew quiet.

"It's that farm raising, girl!" Helen said. Then she gently met Bernice's gaze. Her expression held an unexpected degree of understanding. "Why don't you tell me all about it, honey?"

Bernice's lower lip quivered. As she nodded, a teardrop splashed into her teacup.

Joan's bus squeaked to a halt. She was first to get up. In fact, she was the only one on the bus other than the driver. "See you tomorrow," she called as she opened her umbrella.

At home, Joan noticed a piece of Annie's dime store stationery tucked under a coffee cup placed face down on the kitchen table, with Annie's grade school handwriting. "Joan," it said.

Joan felt sorry for Annie, still working when Joan's work day was all over. It was so much better to have your day free and clear and be home by 2:00 in the afternoon. Poor Annie had to continue on until 4 and sometimes even 5:00. It was starting to get dark earlier, too. At least she didn't open every day.

Then Joan started thinking about what had been dancing around in her heart all day--the weekend retreat! Annie was so good to her. Her salary would never have allowed her to pay for a hotel room, not even half of one. Annie knew that. She could have gone herself, but she knew it was an opportunity that Joan might not otherwise have. Of course, what did Annie need it for? She had Sylvester. He was such a catch. He wasn't quite as romantic as Joan would have liked for herself, but he was very good looking and smart and perfect to Annie. And he had a future. Or at least. . .

Joan's thoughts took her to one of the saddest conversations she and Annie had ever had. One day, when Annie hadn't known Joan was at home, she had come into the house and gone immediately to her room and closed the door. After a few minutes, Joan had gone to the door and knocked hesitantly.

"Annie?"

There had been only silence.

Just as Joan had turned to go, the door had opened and Annie emerged in tears.

"What is it? What's happened!" Joan cried.

"No, no, no!" Annie hushed her, almost whispering. "Nothing's happened, nothing's wrong. I'm. . . I'm sorry Joan, I didn't even know you were here."

"Well if nothing's wrong, then. . ."

They sat at the table. Annie looked down. "It's one of those days," she had said so soulfully that Joan immediately wanted to cry. "Sometimes, Joan, I just think what might happen, you know, if—well, *when* they call up Sylvester for duty. I could lose him."

"Oh Annie, no, don't think that way!" Joan had said, surprised by her own intensity. "There's no reason to believe that will happen. Sylvester is smart. He's not going to let some German capture him!"

"Japanese. . ."

"Or any old Japanese either! Listen, Annie—"

"Italian, Russian—"

Joan put her hands on top of her friend's hands. "Look, he's Italian—they wouldn't take a compadre, and the Russians switched sides, remember? They're allied with us now." She paused. "I know it's hard to keep your imagination from running wild, but you know, it could even turn out that he's *never* called. Did you think of that?"

"I *pray* for that. But I don't believe it."

"Well, you have to do both. And I will, too."

"It's just that Sylvester, he says he doesn't mind. He feels it's his obligation. He's not gung ho like Henry or anything, but he doesn't object, Joan."

Joan had gotten out some graham crackers. "Let's have some of these. You want a glass of milk?"

"Okay."

Joan remembered how she had looked like a little girl, all inward and worried, tear-stained face and twisting fingers. "You really can't blame him for feeling that way, Annie," she said gently. "You should be proud."

"Oh, I am, but I don't—oh I don't really even know what."

"I'd be confused, too," Joan had said. "But we'll get through this together. Okay?"

Annie nodded.

As Joan dropped a cake of soap into the wash basin and sustered through her laundry basket for underwear and socks and her white blouse, she tried to think of other things. Times beyond the War, when Annie and Sylvester would be married, maybe have a baby right away; when Ralph would come home to Helen a war hero, all decorated, and Henry would propose to Bernice, and she, Joan, would, well, she'd have someone. . . Hmm, she thought.

"You get nice and clean, good old laundry," she said out loud. "You might be my only chance!"

After a good scrub, she left the laundry to soak with a little bluing and she decided she had put off reading Annie's note long enough. It was very like Annie to tell important news in a note, Joan thought. She was not one that felt comfortable sharing her deeper feelings. She tried, but she just could not seem to make room for many people deep inside her heart. Joan wasn't that different. A note's okay, thought Joan. I might react better to bad news if there's nobody here. She hoped Annie's parents were all right. She hoped Helen and Bernice were all right. And she hoped that Sylvester was all right.

Making herself sit down, Joan picked up the letter, took a deep breath and began to read.

Dear Joan,

Sorry to write this note, because I know it's not fair to you, but would you please start the tuna casserole at the regular time? I'm going to have to do the inventory and will be a little late.

Your friend,
Annie

Joan dropped the note onto the table. *"Well!"* was all she said.

Outside, two elderly neighbors began their journey to People's Drug for a box of Epsom Salts.

"It's funny how it just suddenly acts up, isn't it, Clara?" asked Rose. "Right out of the blue."

"It's not funny," said Clara, who was in no mood to talk. "It's painful." Clara rubbed her elbow.

"I didn't mean *funny* as in something to laugh about! Goodness gracious, Clara," said Rose, pouting.

"Well. . . I apologize."

"All right, then."

They walked in silence for a few steps. Then Clara said, "It's that granddaughter of mine."

"Oh?" Rose's eyes grew bright and wide. "Did she make something. . . nice. . . for the bazaar?"

"I have no idea. But Pauline says she just up and decided to visit her sister, Kate, in Philadelphia."

"Kate? I didn't know she had a sister named Kate. How old is she?"

"No, no, not *her* sister—"

"But didn't you only just say she decided to up and visit her sister—"

"Pauline's sister! Eh, sorry. Pauline's sister. Her name is Kate. Bernice, she went to go and visit her Aunt Kate in Philadelphia."

"Oh."

They walked for a little while further. And Rose just simply could not resist.

"Well why is that so bad? Bernice visiting her Aunt Kate in Philadelphia? Is she some kind of um, uh, painted lady, maybe?"

Clara sighed. There was no getting around it. Rose would always arrive at the worst possible conclusion. "No," she said patiently. "She's not a painted lady. She's a very respectable widow."

"Well then I don't understand. What's wrong with Bernice's going to visit her Aunt Kate? In Philadelphia?" Rose thought for a moment and then came back with intensely renewed enthusiasm. "Did she go with a *man?*"

"No, she went on a bus. I'm not upset that she went, I'm just confused. What a funny thing to do all of the sudden."

Rose stopped and looked at her friend. "Why don't you ask her?"

Clara stopped, too. She looked suddenly miffed, and said, "Because her mother doesn't want to pry into her business. She doesn't think it's appropriate because Bernice is a grown woman."

"Well," Rose said raising her eyebrows, casually walking once again. "She didn't say *you* couldn't ask her, did she?"

Clara took her friend's arm. "You're right," she said. "She surely didn't!"

Joan rose at 9:30 the next morning, got dressed, finished her packing, found some fresh coffee in the cupboard and started the percolator. It was half hour before Margaret was due to stop by for her. Annie's friend Margaret was 26 and considered an old maid. Joan felt gloomy about going with her on the one hand, because she worried it might bring bad luck. On the other hand, a 26-year-old might make a 21-year-old look very good. Then immediately she felt guilty for thinking that way. She's a nice person to share with me, and even give me a ride with her. What a mean thought to have.

"Good morning," Annie said joining her at the counter. "That coffee smells good!"

"Oh, hi," said Joan.

"Are you nervous?"

"Yes!" Joan giggled. "Very!"

They sat down at the table after getting out some marmalade, put up by Joan's mother, and a couple of slices of bread.

"I would be, too," said Annie. "But try to just think of it as a night out with a nice dinner and a chance to see the ocean."

"I've tried that," said Joan. "I'm trying to convince myself that I do this sort of thing all the time."

They both laughed.

"You're an old pro!" Annie said. "The others'll be coming to you for advice!"

"Well, I thank God for Mom," said Joan, "and my parents' upbringing. Otherwise I would really be nervous. Some people I've seen out in *the world* don't exactly strike me as well-mannered."

"I know exactly what you mean!" said Annie. "But you're right. Your mother is a lady and your father a gentleman."

"And don't forget his constant correcting of grammar!" laughed Joan. "Mommy and *me?*" she said, imitating her father's voice. "Did you say, 'Mommy and *me?*'"

Annie stirred the sugar into her coffee. "It's good they're close by, though," she said. "Makes me feel secure."

"Yeah. And I didn't get any objection about this little outing because it was sponsored by St. Benedict's and because it was your idea."

"Are they up yet?"

"Oh I'm sure of it."

The girls walked into the living room peered across the way into Joan's parents' house's kitchen window. Annie tapped on the window and Joan gave a fluttery little wave.

Through the window, Joan's mother saw them as she stood beside her husband at the kitchen table, a skillet in one hand, a spatula in the other. She dropped some scrambled eggs onto his plate, and waved with the spatula.

"They're really something," said Annie.

Margaret was what many people refer to as a "plain girl." She wore her hair in a pageboy, turned under neatly and a pair of heavy glasses that covered a good deal of her face. She didn't wear any makeup other than lipstick, which was the very wrongest shade of red. But she had a marvelous car.

Joan smiled as she opened the rear door. "Let me just put my things in first," she said. "Good to see you!"

"It's nice to see you, too," Margaret answered, as if reciting lines in a play. "This should be a very nice outing."

Down the street a little ways, Rose stood at her mailbox, watching. She couldn't hear, but she was sure that Joan had just put a suitcase in the back seat. She craned her head to watch as Joan then got into the car, which drove off down the street toward the highway.

"Oh my!" she whispered. "She's running away!"

Annie watched the scene from the front porch and giggled, knowing old Rose would be sure to start up a story going around. That thought brought her back to the funny occurrence the day before with Mrs. St. John. What in the world was that all about, she wondered.

She heard a car horn toot and then Helen's car appeared. "Hello!" Helen called from the road. "I just saw Joan. I hope she has a good time tonight."

"Come on in! Me, too. She deserves it."

As Helen parked the car, Annie fluffed her hair in the mirror and put a tablecloth on the table. "Coffee?" she offered as Helen came in.

"Oh, that sounds wonderful!" Helen answered. "I haven't taken a minute to sit down yet this morning. I've been running errands and you wouldn't believe the line at the grocery store!"

"Oh yes! Saturday's not the day to go there, that's for sure!" Annie said. "I thought you usually went on Thursday mornings."

"I do, but I always forget something. With tomorrow being Sunday, I wanted something nice for dinner. I ended up walking out without a thing."

"Do you have anything? You can eat with me."

"I've got a pork chop, and that's good enough," Helen answered. "Thank you, though. How about if I take a rain check?"

"Fine with me—any time!"

Helen took a sip from a lovely china cup, roses decorating its blended white surface. "Mmm. That's delicious. You make a good cup of coffee, Annie."

Annie laughed. "Okay, I'll take credit for Joan's work!"

"What are you going to do with your day?" Helen asked. "Got any plans?"

"I'm seeing Sylvester this evening," Annie said, her eyes alive. "He's been studying very hard, but he's giving himself a break tonight and we might go to the pictures. I'm not sure. He didn't really say."

"Good for you. I think Bernice is stopping by tonight," said Helen casually.

"Bernice? Really? Is Henry out of town?"

"No, I don't think so. She just said she'd like to stop by, maybe to get out of the house for a while."

"Maybe she wants a chance to put her shell piece together!" Annie laughed.

"Maybe," said Helen. "She's such a sweet girl."

Something in how she'd said that alerted Annie. She looked at Helen, who was gazing into her coffee. "Yeah."

"I don't know about her and shell jewelry, though," said Helen, suddenly back on track.

"It's funny," said Annie. "I haven't seen Bernice, but I've now talked to two people about her."

"Oh?" Helen was suddenly interested.

"Yes."

They sat there for a moment, Helen nodding nonchalantly. Annie continued. "Mrs. St. John was here yesterday. She came out in the pouring rain. She says to me, 'Annie, do you know where Bernice is?' and I said, 'I sure don't, Mrs. St. John.' and of course I worried she was missing or something. It spooked me a little."

"Really?" said Helen.

"Only for a minute," Annie said. "Because as soon as I asked the woman in, she immediately made for the kitchen and sat down."

Helen laughed a merry laugh. "She was after your cheesecake!"

"That's what *I* thought! But I gave her some all the same."

Helen continued to laugh.

"I asked her what was the problem with Bernice, and by the time she'd finished her cake, I swear I think she'd forgotten all about her!"

Helen wiped the corner of her eyes as her laughter came to a stall. "She's a dear old soul, but she is a little. . ."

"Batty!" said Annie with blatant enthusiasm.

Helen began to laugh all over again. "Well," she said, tapering off for the second time, "When I saw Bernice this morning, she was just fine."

"Had she been to her aunt's, been to Philadelphia, then?" Annie asked.

"Oh, she said Philadelphia was beautiful, and that her aunt has a beautiful garden, except that now, of course, it's mostly going to pot with the coming of autumn and all."

"I guess Mrs. St. John thought an eye for an eye."

"How's that, Annie?"

"Her honey cake for Aunt Philomena's cheesecake!"

That night, the autumn moon shone clear and bright, reflected against the black and bouncing background of the Atlantic Ocean. I never get tired of that sight, thought Joan staring out from their balcony window of the Chalfont Hotel. It was only a little bit windy and she'd wanted to breathe in the ocean air just enough to get it into her lungs, but not enough to make her hair frizz up. She stepped inside and looked toward the bathroom. Margaret did take her time, she thought. By the time I get my turn, it will almost be time to meet everyone downstairs.

One hour and 15 minutes after she'd gone into the bathroom, Margaret emerged, looking exactly the same as when she'd gone in.

"How do you like the way I did my hair?" she asked.

"Oh," said Joan charitably, "I like it very much! You have a real knack for doing hair!"

"Thanks," said Margaret, stopping to admire herself in the hallway mirror.   "Well, you'd better hurry and get dressed, Joan. We only have 20 minutes."

Joan sighed, smiled, and carrying her clothing in from the bedroom, she began to dress.

"I sure hope I meet Mr. Right tonight," said Margaret through the door.

"Oh, you never know," said Joan. "He could be down there waiting for you already."

"It could be."

"And maybe mine, too," Joan added.

"Well, I did pay full price to get the room on this trip," said Margaret, as if she were working a mathematical equation. "So I should get dibs on the first one."

"I think my share is fully paid, too," Joan said, confused.

"Oh yeah, it is," Margaret said. "I just meant I was the one who paid. Annie said she was giving you her ticket. And it was a giveaway since she worked in the shop."

Joan took a deep breath and let it out. Margaret was not overly endowed with social graces, she decided, so she would start her rosary now, and just let the little offenses roll off her back. "Let's just try to have a great time, the both of us," she called out cheerfully.

"Yeah," said Margaret. "But don't take forever in there, hear?"

The plan had been set that both groups of young adults would gather in their respective hotels, and then meet on the steps of the Chalfont Hotel. From there they would walk across the way to a Chinese dinner, and then go en masse to the dance at St. Nicholas down the avenue. Since Joan had only to change into her pretty blue and white dress and retouch her makeup, she was ready on time and met up with the other girls in the lobby. She saw several friends of Annie's, and also a few of the girls from choir she'd sung with and one girl whom she'd known from St. Benedict's Girls Academy in grade school.

"Hi Laureen," she greeted her. Laureen wore her hair long in pretty gold coils toward the back of her head, with a golden fold that hung over her forehead as well. She had on a turquoise, chiffon, tea length, like Joan's, and gold and white strappy shoes.

"Joan! I didn't expect to see you here! How are you?" Laureen called out, giving her friend a little hug.

"Me neither 'til yesterday! Annie said I should go since she's not looking," she paused and smiled raising her eyebrows, "and she thought it might be a good opportunity for me to get out and meet some people."

"Oh yeah, *people*," laughed Laureen.

"Of the male persuasion," added Joan. "How about you? You look gorgeous!"

"Oh, thank you! And I'm here to have a good time, but I'm afraid I'm spoken for." She held up her left hand. "As of last month."

"Laureen! It's gorgeous," said Joan, admiring her diamond ring. "Congratulations."

"It'll be you soon enough, Joan," Laureen answered kindly. "You look out of this world fantastic."

"Thanks," Joan said.

Just then Margaret made her way to Joan. Tapping her on the shoulder a little boyishly, she said, "Aren't you going to introduce me to your friend?"

"Oh of course. Laureen, this is Margaret. She works with Annie at St. Benedict's."

"Well, I don't work *with* Anne, to be exact," Margaret corrected. "I work as an office aid and delivery girl for the office at St. Benedict's. Strictly speaking, Anne isn't an employee of St. Benedict's."

"I see," said Laureen warmly. "It's nice to meet you, Margaret."

"Likewise."

Just then a tall elderly woman with her hair in a tight bun and a clipboard under her arm signaled for their attention, clapping her hands, and calling out, "Girls! Girls! May I have your attention please?"

Everyone turned in her direction.

"My name, for those of you who do not know me, is Mrs. Lewis. I will be your matron and in charge of the girl chaperones. We will soon exit the lobby *en masse*, and assemble on the steps. Let's let those boys get a good look!"

The large, echoey lobby erupted in giggles as 28 girls, between the ages of 18 and 26, let loose a little nervous tension.

"Everyone is to behave according to the Code of Behavior for good Catholic girls," she continued, "and I and our other matrons will be around. So no funny business or side trips to any closets or dark hallways. We *will be watching*. The main thing is to meet and pair with a nice man. Remember these are the cream of the crop, good respectable men who will make good husbands and fathers. And if you strike out this time, there's always next time. And as always, have a grand evening!"

All the girls clapped, some of them batting away tears of anticipation or just plain nerves.

They filed out through the doors held open by porters attired in Dickensian dress, and assembled as directed on the long, gracious stairway, waiting for the men from the hotel across the way to group together.

"Stick with me, kid," Laureen said. "I'll find you a good one."

"I'm as nervous as a kitten," Joan said. "You better believe I'll stick with you."

"Maybe Bob even knows someone," Laureen said.

Then suddenly the doors of the Wayside opened. It stood on ground level. A trickle of young men inched out, followed by a sudden bunching of others rapidly crossing the avenue in uneven progression toward the Chalfont. Some were looking at each other, while others were pretending to be distracted by the nonexistent traffic. And there were a few who, knowing a good opportunity when it came along, were looking over the lovely ladies as if they had just set foot into the gates of Heaven.

"That's my Bob," said Laureen, elbowing Joan.

Joan didn't react.

"Hear me?" Laureen repeated. "That's my knight in shining armor."

But Joan didn't see Bob. She didn't see anyone but the tall, dark-haired man striding meaningfully in her direction it seemed. Their eyes met for a few seconds and Joan thought she would faint.

"Joanie!" Laureen said, getting into her face. "Oh! Sorry!" she said, laughing. Then turning to where Joan was looking, she saw what Joan saw; a gorgeous fellow heading directly toward them, and then. . . suddenly. . . not.

A tiny, bubbly redhead had appeared out of nowhere, right in front of Joan's man and had, by some mysterious and devastating means, drawn him completely off course.

"What the--!" Laureen exclaimed. "Why, that little b—"

"No, no, that's okay," said Joan. She was blinking as fast as she could to work out the tears before they welled up in her pretty blue eyes.

"You've got to be joking," said Laureen, incensed on Joan's behalf. "He was headed right to you, looking right at you! He was looking right *at* you!"

"Hey look, here's someone coming for you," Joan said, purposefully distracting her, and trying to distract herself as well. "Is this Sir Galahad?"

"What—oh yes, Bob! Hello darling," she said, reaching out to a well-built, redheaded fellow of about twenty-two. "And Bob McGarrett, this is my friend, Joan. We went to St. Benedict's together."

"Hello, Joan," Bob said, embracing Laureen. "Nice to meet you."

"Hello, Bob," said Joan. "You've got a keeper, there."

Laureen smiled at Joan. "Don't I know it," Bob answered.

By then, the two groups were mingling and Mrs. Lewis was beckoning for everyone to follow her and the chaperones into the well-appointed Chinese Palace only a couple of doors down the avenue.

"We'll sit together, okay Joan? Okay, Bob?" said Laureen, bouncing up and down as they walked.

Joan nodded. Tears of frustration were welling in her eyes against her best efforts, and she didn't want to make any more motions than necessary, as she tried to keep them in place.

But she wasn't fooling Laureen. "Oh, Joanie!" she whispered grabbing her arm. "Don't you worry, that old Jezebel's not getting him!

At the word "Jezebel," Joan felt an uncontrollable urge to giggle and started jiggling her tears, which were suddenly meaningless, sending them splashing onto her perfect complexion.

"Come *on*, Joan, I'm not kidding," said Laureen, looking very serious.

"Okay, okay, thanks," said Joan, just grateful that she was no longer at tears' door.

They arrived at a round table covered with a bright red tablecloth. As they seated themselves, waiters in white coats handed out menus.

"What in tarnation is a *pupu* platter?" asked Bob, breaking the silence.
Laureen and Joan giggled.

"I don't know," said Laureen, "but I don't think I'll have any."

"Oh no, it's nice," said Joan. "I've seen pictures of those in the magazines."

"Well, I've seen pictures, too," said Bob, "but I wouldn't call it 'nice.'"
Joan laughed. Bob winked at Laureen.

"Seriously," Joan went on, "it comes with a little candle or something in the middle, and it's lit, like a flame, and then around it, you have all kinds of different little hors d'Oeuvres, little barbecued ribs, something they call shrimp toast, oh all kinds of good things!"

Just then, Mrs. Lewis began to signal from the center of the restaurant. "Excuse me Ladies and Gentlemen. I see nearly everyone has found a seat. Excellent. Now you were given menus by your very attentive waiters." She sent a patient smile over to the cluster of Oriental waiters standing by the kitchen.

"However, you will not need the menus. As you know, your dinner is included in this little excursion, and as such we have arranged a choice of two main dishes, a soup, and an appetizer. Your waiter will come around, collect the menus, and begin taking orders very soon. We have only 45 short minutes to enjoy this lovely dinner before the orchestra begins to play in the lobby of St. Nick's, so we must make quick decisions and not dally around our dinners too long. Waiters?"

"Well," said Laureen closing her menu. "I guess she put the kibosh on that."

"Yeah," said Bob, "you might say she poo-pooed it."

The girls giggled and Joan started to ask Laureen what she thought the two choices might be when she felt someone tap her on the shoulder.

"E'cuse me, Miss," the waiter said, "you havvah pawk or a cheekin?"

Laureen turned to see the Chinese waiter who leaned over her with a pencil and pad. She looked back at Bob and Joan, her eyebrows raised. Joan shook her head.

"Pardon me?" asked Bob.

"You havva poke or *cheeee*ken?" inquired the waiter, taking great pains to pronounce the last word.

"Well. . ." Bob began.

"I believe he's trying to ascertain what you want to have for dinner," came a warm, friendly voice behind Joan, "the pork, or the chicken?" Everyone turned to see Tall, Dark & Handsome standing there, chuckling lightly.

"Hi Dick!" said Bob. He stood up to greet him warmly as Joan and Laureen exchanged glances, astonished. "Grab a seat, Bud, we've got room."

"Well, actually I've got myself situated over there," he indicated a few tables over, "but I came over to say hello, and to meet uh, your friends." He turned to look at Joan.

Joan stopped breathing.

"Sure," said Bob, oblivious to the goings on around him. "This lovely lady," he rested his hand on her shoulder, "is Laureen, and her friend from school over there is Joan."

"Hello," both girls said at once.

Laureen laughed. "That's how they trained us at school," she said. Everyone laughed.

"Joan! Okay, finally I found you!" bellowed Margaret, who had just arrived and was madder than a hornet. She took a chair right next to Joan and hissed,   "Thanks a lot for dumping me!"

"Oh Margaret, I'm so sorry! I guess I just thought you'd wound up with someone else."

"Hi Margaret," Laureen said, holding out her hand, "This is Bob and this is Dick, Bob's friend."

Margaret shook his hand gracelessly while looking down at the table. "Margaret Camp." She nodded to everyone else without actually looking anyone in the eye, her pageboy accentuating her serious expression.

Dick exchanged glances with Bob. "Well, it's awfully nice meeting you all," he said. "I guess I'd better amble on back to my table before they come around for orders. I don't want to get stuck with some doughy thing for dinner."

Joan tried hard to stifle a giggle. Her amusement was not lost on Dick, as he looked her way and smiled. "I hope you'll save me a dance," he said.

"I will," said Margaret.

To which Joan giggled again.

"What?" said Margaret.

"Scuse me," said the waiter, "you a wanna ckeeeekin?

Chapter Four

Annie hung up the phone. She held her hand to the receiver, and her eyes on her hand. "Maybe if I'd gone to the dance instead of pawning it off on Joan. Maybe if I'd gone in to the shop today. Maybe if Helen had come over and, well she did, but maybe if I'd gone somewhere with her, or . . ." As her voice trailed off, she lifted her hand off the phone as if it required great concentration, knowing that the news was no less real if she'd continued to hold onto the telephone receiver. She let if drop stiffly at her side, and exhaled heavily. She stood for another moment, looking around room, as if she were trying to find a place to hide. Or a space she could neatly fit into. Somewhere she could burrow in and become one with the structure. Apart from herself, and part of something else.

Then just as her desperation began to turn to tears, a knock came on the door.

Oh! she thought, if that Mrs. St. John is here again, I'll—she opened the door with a jerk, but instead found the warm and comforting form of Helen. Instantly, Annie let herself fall into a rubble of heart wrenching tears.

"Oh, dear, dear," said Helen, stepping inside and gently taking charge. "Come on over here, now, and sit down." She walked Annie over to the sofa. "Sit down, honey," she said. "Just have your cry. There's nothing better for it than a good, honest cry."

By the time the kettle started to scream, Annie was about done doing her own version of that.

"I'll make us a pot," said Helen, patting Annie on the hand.

"I should have gone out today," said Annie joining Helen at the stove. "Not that it would have changed things. Everything would still be the same, but at least, well, it would have been later."

Helen paused, tea kettle in mid-air. "Sylvester got called up, did he, Honey?"

Annie nodded, her big brown eyes swollen and her fine boned face blotchy from dried tears.

"Oh honey," said Helen shaking her head and pouring the tea. "I know it seems like the end of the world, but Sylvester is a smart man. They're not going to put him in a dangerous spot. They'll want him behind the lines, working on strategy, or planning maneuvers."

"Do you think so?" asked Annie earnestly, looking more like a little girl than Helen could ever remember seeing her.

"Oh heavens yes, he's not a foot soldier type."

They sat at the kitchen table in silence for a few minutes and then Helen got up to close the curtains. "Are we in blackout this week?" she asked.

"I don't know, they've got the dance on at the shore."

"Oh yes, the dance," she said. Helen's heart was heavy as she turned to find the can of tea. "Will you see Sylvester before he goes?"

"Yes, tomorrow, for a little while," said Annie, "and then in three days, when I see him off." She sighed. "I tried, Helen, but there is no way to prepare for this."

"No," said Helen. "There isn't."

The hall at St. Nicholas, which backed up against the church and rectory, was decorated with big bunches of artificial flowers. And while it was clear the flowers themselves had seen better days, they had been so well arranged in combination with the long, sparkling streamers and colorful little lanterns holding bouquets of miniature roses that the guests were transported instantly as they walked through the doorway.

The orchestra had set up under an expanded length of sheeting, made festive with glitter and clusters of lights. The word that had been circulating was that a couple members of Artie Shaw's band were still in town and were "sitting in" with the local orchestra for the night.

Laureen took Joan's hand. "Let's go and sit at that table," she said. "It won't be too loud, and we'll be really close to the dance floor. I just know Bob'll bring Dick over!"

"Okay," Joan fairly whispered. "Gee, Laureen, you're so nice to help me out like this," she said squeezing her hand.

"Are you kidding? Us gals gotta stick together!" Laureen answered. "But seriously, I'm so happy and

I want to spread it around. Besides, Dick is *so* smitten."

Joan's eyes brightened. "Do you really think so?"

"Oh yes!" Laureen giggled. "The bit about saving a dance for him at the table, and Margaret responding—Hey, where is she, by the way?"

"Oh golly, Laureen—I don't know! Let's look for her."

"Yeah, but the table—we need to save the table. Look, I'll go and look for her, you sit here."

"Do you remember what she looks like?"

"Yes, pink dress, pageboy hair, glasses."

"And about my height."

"Okay, Joan. I'm on my way. Just sit and wait."

The band was getting situated inside the tight space reserved for them. The telling sounds of a falling music stand or collapsed folding chair could be heard, followed by unrecognizable oaths of anger. Joan was just beginning to feel a little displaced when she spotted Dick only a few steps away.

"Hello again," he said.

Joan froze up, startled. "Uh. . ." she began.

"Dick! Oh Dick! There you are!" called a very petite, very pretty redhead in a screechy voice. Her high heels click-clacked against the wooden floor with pert little struts. "I was wondering what happened to you." She paused to give Joan the visual once over. "Mmph," she snorted, obviously not considering her to be serious competition. She turned and cozied up to Dick. *"We,"* she paused, checking Joan out of the corner of her eye, "are other *there.*"

Joan fought to keep from reacting. She smiled, not knowing what else to do. Dick retreated into the sea of candlelit tables.

Just then, Laureen, Bob, and Margaret arrived. The room was rapidly filling and the band had begun to play.

Laureen caught Joan's eye. "What's going on?" she seemed to be asking.

Annie sat by the phone, her hand and eyes still on it from her latest call with Sylvester. She was calmer now. The sting was still there but somehow the long months of preparation and waiting had lightened the burden for when the time had actually arrived. For Sylvester, too.

"You know, Annie, I think I'm practically prepared for this, what with the signing up and all and seeing so many guys ahead of me get called. I'm just glad I got my exams done at mid-term. I don't think I'll have to start the semester over when I get back."

"Too bad they can't mail you your assignments," Annie joked. "Maybe you could get your sergeant to type them up for you."

"*My* sergeant? Huh. I'll be lucky if I make sergeant myself."

"I think they're putting college guys in as lieutenant," said Annie.

"Yeah? Where'd you hear that?"

"Some gals were talking in the shop today. Of course I would have paid more attention if I'd known. . . " her voice trailed off.

"I know Sweetie," Sylvester said, his voice skipping just a little.

Then both were silent for a while. Annie could hear a siren somewhere in the background on Sylvester's end.

"Let's not run up your bill," she said bravely. "We'll see each other tomorrow."

"Yep, tomorrow," he said, trying to sound upbeat.

And after they'd said goodbye, Annie had just sat. First she prayed the Chaplet, and then just sat, thinking of Sylvester, wanting him safely home already.

"But I know You will watch over him," she said softly aloud. The artist's rendition of the Sacred Heart in its wooden frame seemed to smile right into her soul. She felt secure, and then suddenly light-hearted.

She stood up, gathered up the dishes she and Helen had used and started for the sink. She washed up everything and started drying the cups when she spotted a young housefly that had fallen into the rinse water. She tried but just simply could not ignore the little creature. She grabbed a wide butter knife from the utensil drawer and slowly lowered it under the fly so as not to create a mini tidal wave around it, and then raised it up and set the knife benignly on the counter. For a few seconds the fly did nothing but lay there, a wad of wet wings and legs.

Annie picked up her towel and continued drying the cups, keeping an eye on her little beneficiary. After a couple minutes, it seemed as if life was returning.

"Here I am, Mr. Clean, and I'm trying to save your life," she said chuckling. "I hope you recover and do a good deed in return."

As if the fly had understood, he raised himself up a little, and flexed his rapidly drying wings. He fluttered, and initiated takeoff proceedings. The first effort was a short flight from the knife's edge to the edge of the sink. But then he paused, recharged his tiny little batteries, lifted off and buzzed Annie's right ear before exiting for places unknown.

"Yeah, you're welcome," Annie said. She yawned and decided it wasn't too early to think about getting ready for bed. Sylvester's news was something she'd rather not think about any longer than necessary. So she flicked off the kitchen lights when suddenly there was a hard bang bang *bang!* on the front door.

Annie froze in place. What in the world? It couldn't be Sylvester. Gosh, she thought, I hope it's not Joan coming home early in defeat.

"Well I'm not answering it unless I know who it is," she muttered to herself.

And almost as if she'd shouted it out, a voice rang out in response. "Annie, open the door! It's me. And it's freezing out here!"

Annie flew to the door. "What are you doing out so late?" she asked, completely forgetting herself.

"Well," said Bernice. "Nice to see you, too!"

Annie laughed. "Sorry! Come in, come in!"

"Thanks," said Bernice. "I'm stayin' over."

"Okay."

"Do you have coffee?"

"Coffee? Not exactly—you want tea?"

"No, that's all right," said Bernice, plopping onto the couch. "But I'll take the sympathy."

"Ha," said Annie. "You're not gettin' any from me."

"Why not?"

"Well until I have a better understanding about all this mystery," Annie said, "you're not gettin' nothin'!"

Bernice smirked. "Cute," she said. "So I get mysterious, you divert to your downtowner vernacular."

"It's not *downtownER*," said Annie, "it's *downtown*."

"No er?"

"No."

"Okay, so until you—"

"Never mind!" said Annie, half exasperated and half joking. "Where the dickens have you been?"

"Look, I'm here now. What's the diff?"

"Oooh, you've got some hot vernacular there yourself, Miss Get About Town."

"Everybody says 'what's the diff,'" shot Bernice. "It's not downtowner."

"Oh my gosh! Down*town*!"

"Yeah, yeah, yeah," said Bernice nodding and looking around the place.

"Seriously," Annie said, taking a seat beside her on the couch, the kitchen towel still in her hand. "What are you up to these days? You've got everybody confused and concerned."

"Look," said Bernice, "I think some people might do better refraining from inserting their nasal passages into someone else's business."

Annie burst out laughing. "Nasal passages?" And she laughed again, in fact, so hard that Bernice couldn't help joining in. They went on for some time, stopping and then starting up all over again. Finally Annie, wiping her eyes, said, "Thanks—you don't know how much I needed that."

"Oh yes I do," said Bernice. "That's why I'm here."

"What do you mean?"

"Helen told me all about it. I know you're going through a rough time, and with Joan at the lovers' weekend—"

Annie laughed again. "She's just at a dance—"

"I know, but I really feel like this is her weekend," Bernice said.

"Well I hope you're right!"

"Anyway, I didn't want you to be alone."

Annie gave her a hug. "You are so sweet. Thanks. I was just going to hit the hay but now you're here, what do you say we play a game?"

"Okay," said Bernice. "That sounds good to me. I've got my knitting in my handbag, but it looks more like a rat's nest than a hat."

"Oh come on," Annie said, patting her friend's hand.

Bernice smiled, accepting the comfort she thought she was getting.

"You've never seen a rat's nest," Annie continued.

"No, I *haven't!*" Bernice said, not amused. "It's a figure of speech. And thanks a lot."

"I'm just trying to be witty," Annie chuckled. "Seriously though, Bernice, you can get it. Just keep trying."

"I think anybody can eventually get it right," Bernice said thoughtfully. "It's just, I'm not really sure I want to all that badly."

"No, but when you and Henry tie the knot, you'll have to know—"

"*If.*"

"What?"

"If we tie the knot."

Annie's eyes shot open wide. She pulled back and gave her friend a full appraisal. "I knew it!" she said.

"Knew what?"

"I knew you were seeing somebody else—that story about your aunt in Philly--"

"Hey, my aunt *does* live in Philly and I did go there," said Bernice defiantly.

"But you *are* seeing someone else?"

Bernice just shook her head and looked toward the cheerful curtains hung at the window for a moment. "Tonight," she said solemnly, "I've come to see you in what I thought might be your hour of need."

Annie drew back, mystified, seeing a totally new side of Bernice. She felt an unfamiliar level of respect for her. "Sure, Bernie, okay," she said. "I really appreciate it."

They sat there silently for a couple minutes until Bernice said, "So what game do you want to play?"

"How about cards? Gin or something?"

"Crazy Eights?"

"Yeah, great," said Annie. "So we'll have tea, sympathy, and cards." She got up to get things set up.

"Okay, but the sympathy's supposed to be for you."

The light in the hallway outside Joan and Margaret's room at the hotel was dim and yellowy and it bore nowhere near the promise it had just 3 hours before. Joan fished through her pocketbook for what remained of the handkerchief, soppy with tears, and as best as she could figure, a Manhattan.

"Here, I've got one," Laureen said. "It's just paper, though."

"Thanks," said Joan.

"Do you have your key?"

"Yeah, it's right here." Joan opened the door. The room was still welcoming but it seemed somehow smaller and less grand.

"Oh look at that view of the ocean!" cried Laureen. "That's breathtaking."

"It sure is," said Joan.

Laureen looked around. "Are you sure you don't have anything you can switch into? How about just a plain black dress?"

"Nope, nothing," said Joan. "I didn't plan on playing catcher for a flying beverage!"

Laureen giggled. "Oh Joan, thank God! You are so good to see the humor in it!"

Joan sighed, and sat down looking at the front of her dress. It was stained and still very wet. "Gosh, I could get drunk on just the smell of that."

Laureen giggled again. "I think maybe she was!"

"Do you really think so?"

"No, not really. But I don't know if I buy that it was an accident."

"Who knows?" said Joan. "Either way, she got what she was after." She began to feel a little morose again.

"Oh no she didn't. Dick left," said Laureen defiantly.

"He did?" said Joan, brightening.

"Yep, as soon as you left, Redhead began to make her play. But he looked at his watch and said something like oh, I have get some sleep or something, and he left."

"Well that's something."

"It sure is!"

"But he doesn't have my number," she paused. "He didn't even ask me for it."

Laureen sighed. "I know." She stood up to look out the window. "Hey, but he's not a stranger. Remember, Bob knows him."

"You think he'll ask?"

"I'm sure he will!" she said turning around. "Hey, just think, you found yourself a good guy, had a nice dinner, and did it all in just a couple hours. That usually takes weeks, months!"

"And I planned it just that way," said Joan, chuckling.

"Oh I know," said Laureen. "You coordinated it just perfectly. How did you get her to spill that on you? Was that how you got around paying for the drink?"

They laughed like school girls.

Just then the door shot open and Margaret stood there, her face squinched up and her eyebrows knit together. "What in the *world* happened to you?" she demanded, looking at Joan. "Did you fall in the fountain?"

"Joan was playing catcher to a phantom highball," said Laureen.

"Huh, no kidding," said Margaret. "And I thought *I* was the one who wasn't so refined." She shook her head as she headed for her room. Laureen and Joan started giggling again. "It's not that funny," shot Margaret, shutting her door.

On the following Monday morning, Annie sat with Joan and Helen in the second pew at St. Benedict's, listening to the choir at the offertory.

"I'm surprised the choir is here for Armistice Day," Joan whispered.

"I think it's because of the way things are going," Helen whispered back. "Father wants us to stay positive."

The gentle sounds of Panis Angelicus filtered through the wide and echoey chambers of the building, in rich layers, nourishing souls and soothing hearts. The hymn always brought tears to Annie's eyes for its beauty and hope. She thought of Sylvester. How would she ever say goodbye to him?

Father Bertrand raised the Host. As he genuflected before the consecrated bread, Annie lowered her head in prayer. "Please God," she prayed silently, "watch over him. Watch over all the men."

Chapter Five

At Helen's the following Thursday afternoon, Joan arrived before the other girls, as usual. She and Helen chatted as she laid the table. Helen cleaned some celery and carrots.

"Unless Bernice comes through with another cake this week," she said, "I'm afraid it's going to be slim pickings."

"Sorry we didn't get our goodies this week," said Joan. "I'm not sure what happened, but I think Annie said they were having trouble with one of the trucks, so they didn't want to go out too far until they got it repaired. They only make a stop for us on their way up to Pomona, so if they're not going there, they don't come to Mom's."

"That's okay," said Helen. "We can afford to sacrifice a little with all our boys—" She looked up at Joan. "How's Annie doing?"

Joan shook her head. "I'm amazed," she said. "Since she said goodbye to him Tuesday night, I have not heard a word about him. And I don't dare ask."

"That's probably wise," agreed Helen. "When she wants to talk about it, Annie will be sure to let us know."

As if on cue, there was a knock on the door. "Okay, open up in there! This is a raid!" called Bernice.

Helen raised her hands over her head as Joan opened the door.

"See, look you scared her, you idiot," said Annie to Bernice.

"Yeah, she looks really scared," said Bernice.

"Take whatever I have, it's yours, just don't take my shells," said Helen.

"We're not the bad guys," said Bernice. "We're the cops."

"Oh. Well, then I give myself up."

Bernice shook her head and rolled her eyes.

"Pretty pathetic law enforcers if you ask me," said Joan. "Aren't you supposed to have a height requirement? How did a pipsqueak like you get on the squad?"

"Put 'em up. Come on, I dare ya to take a swing at me, come on!" Bernice said, dancing around like a deranged boxer.

Joan and Annie were laughing so hard, Annie fell into a chair and Joan fell trying to keep her from falling.

"How about some coffee, gals?" called Helen, heading to the kitchen. "No goodies today, but we got fresh crunchies."

"I beg to differ," said Bernice. "Guess who picked up 6 raised doughnuts from the diRosa Family Bakery this afternoon?"

"Bernice! No kidding," said Helen. "Good for you."

"No! Not Bernice," Annie said, getting to her feet and heading for Bernice. "Annie, that means *me*, went for them, thank you very much."

"Ah six of one, half dozen of another," said Bernice.

"We'll have the half dozen," said Annie, "you can have what's left."

"Did you guys remember we have to come up with two covered dishes for next Friday, the boys at USO?" asked Joan as she took her customary seat next to Helen.

"I did remember, then I forgot again. We have to figure all that out," said Annie.

"Well, I'll be hostessing," said Helen. "I may bring some cookies, though."

"What do young men want to eat when they're away from home?" Joan asked. "I mean besides their mom's cooking?"

"I've heard fried chicken," said Helen, "and that's an easy one to do. Time-consuming, but not too costly, especially if you've been saving your lard."

"That's a good idea, Helen. I think I'll see if can do that. Make a whole basket full."

"They'll run straight for it," said Annie smiling. "Maybe we should both make fried chicken."

"No, well, if she makes the fried chicken," Helen said, "maybe you can make a few sheets of corn bread, and just cut it in squares."

"Well what do I do?" Bernice asked, beginning to feel left out.

"They'll need a really nice punch," said Helen, "and we're always running short on cups. Maybe you can put together a nice big punch and try to round up some extra tumblers."

Bernice seemed satisfied with her assignment.

"Oh!" she said. "Let me at those doughnuts!"

There was a chill in the air as Annie and Joan got into Annie's car.

"Helen seemed very at ease tonight," said Annie. "I don't know how she does it."

"She says she takes her solace right there at St. Benedict's," Joan said. "I'm sure it must work miracles for people in her situation."

Annie leaned against her car door before opening it. "It does," she said, her voice cracking. Joan looked up, startled. "It's the only place," Annie went on, "that I truly feel like there is hope, that he'll make it out alive." She put her head against the car door and sobbed.

Quickly Joan ran to her, surprised to see that falter, that chink in the armor, that revealed so much Annie would prefer to keep inside, but under those new and terrifying circumstances, could not. Joan wanted so much to protect her from it, guard her heart for her.

"I don't know if I can take it," she sobbed. "It feels like my heart is literally ripping in half."

"Oh Annie, I'm so sorry," was all Joan could say.

Back at home, Joan hung up their jackets. "So far," she said, "he's still Stateside for now. Maybe he'll be put to work here, and not even have to go overseas."

"I don't know how it all works," said Annie, "but because he's more of an engineer, I mean, that's what he's studying anyway, they are more likely to need him in Europe."

Joan felt her heart breaking for her friend. She was such a strong girl, woman. If this was dogging her this badly, it was a place Joan did not want to be. I would just wither up and die in the same circumstances, she thought.

By the time they called it a day, Annie was back to her upbeat, fun-loving self. They had gotten out all of their crafts, trying to come up with new ideas for Helen's marvelous shells.

"Bernice's project even looks like something now," said Annie.

"What do you think it looks like?" said Joan.

"A big clump of shells," said Annie, giggling.

Bernice opened her small bag, happy to be back to that room. She opened the top drawer to the wide, cedar bureau. The scent of the wood rose, rich tones right to her heart, swelling with the olfactory pleasure and the giddiness of once again returning to this place. An old-fashioned porcelain basin sat brightly at a corner table, its blue and white pattern a joy to Bernice's eyes.

Is that what they call "wedgeward?" she thought. It's so gentle and calming. This place is like a slow moving shallow river in summer with ducks on top and soft sand and pebbles at the bottom. Oh, how I wish Annie could be here.

But the thought left her quickly as she heard the familiar footsteps in the hall, and the tap-tap-tap on each of the doors of the rooms around her. "Supper!" a cheerful voice called out. Bernice quickly put her things away, grabbed her rosary case, and joined the others in the hall.

Joan put down the phone. No answer at all at Bernice's house. She wanted to talk to her about Annie, maybe make a plan for how they could cheer her up, do something special for her on Sunday. Bernice may not be good with arts and crafts, but she was a little powerhouse when it came to ideas. All Joan knew is that her dear friend, the one who always buoyed her spirits, was suffering and that she wanted to help.

"You can't always help," her mother had said. "Sometimes people need these times to grow. They probably appreciate everything you do, but they have to go through it themselves."

Joan understood that, but still she wanted to be there for her friend. She thought of all the times through the previous year when Annie had said just the right thing, or taken the time to set up a nice tea and cookies or cake; she thought of the times she had tried to find her a nice man—oh my gosh, thought Joan suddenly. I haven't thought about Dick all evening! I guess I *can* think of someone besides myself for once. She laughed out loud, then quickly stifled herself. Annie's going to think I've gone around the bend, she thought. But oh, I do hope I see that man again, and soon. He *must* remember me, be thinking about me at least somewhat. Laureen said he left right after I did. That must mean he didn't see any point in staying at the dance any longer if I wasn't there. Or maybe he was just tired, or worse, thought the whole thing was stupid or something. He seemed so sophisticated, being from Washington, D.C. and all. Oh, I can't worry about it tonight, though. I'll just have to be as patient as I can, and concentrate on Annie for now.

Just a bedroom door away, Annie closed her eyes and cradled memories of those last precious moments with Sylvester.

It had been one of those misty early fall evenings and she hadn't known whether to wear a sweater or a jacket. Joan had encouraged her to take a jacket so she was looking through the pockets and she found a holy card of St. Joseph, with the prayer for warriors on the opposite side. It had been one she'd picked up in the vestibule of St. Benedict's only a month or two before. Father Bertrand often offered small gifts to his congregation in these beautiful reminders of those who were looking for them.

Annie put the card back in the pocket, slipped the jacket on and met Sylvester at the door ten minutes later. They'd gone to the diner. It was inexpensive, good, and it didn't take long to get served. It was also a warm and familiar place that both of them loved. The lights were high and people were cheerful and talkative.

"I'll never get over how these folks can cook up something this good, this fast," Sylvester said, enjoying his pot roast and egg noodles. "Just incredible."

"It already mostly cooked," Annie said, "they got it ready and just have to keep it hot or heat it up quick in the oven when you order it."

"Not these noodles," he said. "They just made 'em."

"Yeah, you're right. I guess they got the water boiling. Ready and waiting."

"That's more than I can say for me," Sylvester said quietly.

"Me, too," said Annie.

"I'm glad you got to meet my mom," he said. "It's good you got her phone number."

"Yeah, and she's got mine. Maybe we can get together if we get enough rations for the trip."

He took her hand as he'd done 1000 times before. "Don't never think I forgot ya. I'll be back."

"Don't you worry. I aint gonna let ya!" Annie responded, her North Jersey vernacular matching his word for word.

"I mean it," he said, squeezing her hand. "I got no idea what they want with me, but whatever they got in mind, I'll be back."

"I'll be here waitin'," she said. "Don't let me down."

"No. I won't do that." But it sounded more like "I won't do dat."

"Well," Annie said, reaching into her pocket, "just to be sure, I got something for you." She handed him the holy card. "You see that prayer? That's for you. And your buddies—the ones you don't even know yet. It's a prayer for warriors, to St. Joseph. It was written around 55 AD, and it never fails the faithful."

"Let me see that," Sylvester said.

"Keep it in a safe place, okay?"

"Always," he said, looking at the card and then carefully putting it in his wallet. "I won't never let it leave my sight."

Annie laughed. "You just did!"

He hugged her then, hiding tears welling in his eyes. "I love your laugh," he said. "I know I'm just a kid in school, but when you laugh, I feel like the luckiest man alive."

Annie was glad that they hadn't parted at the train station as so many other young couples had, because it was sitting together with him in the diner she recalled, not standing on a cold platform, filled with "weepers," as Bernice called them. But she had always wondered at his statement—that he was just a kid in college. How did he know that he didn't know so much? That was wisdom, she thought. That doesn't come easy. There's a lot about this guy I just don't know yet. And Lord, she prayed, I really want to. Please keep him safe.

She drifted into a deep and peaceful sleep for the first time in months.

Chapter Six

"I knew we were going to get this soppy stuff when it turned cold yesterday," said Bernice. She handed Helen the damp dishtowel. "It always rains after a cold spell in fall."

"You're getting pretty good with the quick dish drying," Helen said. "Been practicing?"

They laughed. "Yeah, I get up early in the morning," Bernice said, "and I line them up out back then grab a dishtowel and go to it!"

"I'm happy to see you happy," Helen said, and gave her a little hug. "And I'm so happy that I know you."

Bernice was startled. "Well that came out of nowhere!"

Helen smiled and arranged the dishtowel on the oven handle so that it could dry quickly. "Not really," she said. "I've been thinking it for a while."

"Thanks," Bernice said. They stared at the floor for a few seconds before familiar knocking on the front door brought a break in the tension. "Here come the troops!"

Annie and Joan had bought the chicken, and Helen offered to supply the fat. "I hope you can't taste the fish fry," she said. "I only used a little of it for that."

"I don't think those men will care one way or the other," said Joan. "Fried chicken is fried chicken."

"How many are there supposed to be?" Annie asked, settling her bags of chicken into the sink. "Oh you've got such a nice, deep sink."

"Thanks, and good thing. You girls have brought piles of chicken! And I don't know how many, but I did hear," she stopped to catch Bernice's eye, "that there may be boys brought in from the Catholic group again, the one in the DC area."

Joan looked up with a jerk. Bernice burst out laughing. "I knew that would get you," she said.

Joan giggled nervously. "How do you know?" she asked Helen.

"Bernice heard it, not me."

Joan grabbed Bernice by both arms. "Tell me! Come on, what did you hear? Tell me!"

"Here Joanie, I'll help you," said Annie, "we'll tickle it out of her!"

"No, no!" laughed Bernice. "I'll tell!" She caught her breath and sat down. "Mom said that Grandma Clara said she heard that the dinner dance went so well that they wanted to invite those same groups as before, give them more opportunities before they ship out. I don't know for sure if the same fellas will come, but I think they all would have been told about it. I think, anyway."

"So they're coming to the USO dance here, at St. Benedict's?"

"Well," said Annie, "if you think about it, it makes sense. The hall is huge, bigger than St. Nick's in town, and it's only 10 minutes into town—"

"Maybe 10 if *you're* driving," interrupted Bernice.

"Okay, okay," said Annie, "but you get the picture. They can stay at the rooming house across from the Chalfont or something, but come to our dances."

"Dance, singular," said Helen. "For many of them, this will be their last before they ship out."

"Oh, thank you voice of doom!" said Bernice.

"Well, I'm just saying all the more reason why they'd invite these fellows back. Were they a nice group, Joan?"

"Oh, I think Joan thinks they were nice!" Annie said, laughing.

Joan smiled and sighed. "Yes, very nice. I'm trying to stay calm. Oh, if only I had Laureen's telephone number, I could see what she knows."

"Margaret!" said Annie.

"Margaret?"

"Yeah. She would know, I bet anything. She's always got the news. By the way, she said she met someone that Saturday, too."

"You're kidding!" said Joan.

"No," Annie said. "Apparently he—"

"I hate to interrupt this important News Bulletin," said Helen, "but if you two don't stop chewing the fat and start heating the fat, you're not going to have any chicken for those hungry fellows to appreciate."

Around the corner and a few doors down, Rose knocked upon Clara's door and opened it. "May I come in, Clara?"

"Well you're already in, for heaven's sakes, yes, then, come on in."

"Oh my, what are you doing?"

"What does it look like I'm doing? I've got the most painful corn. Here, I guess I'm finished. Help me dump the tub."

Rose set down her suitcase-sized pocketbook and helped Clara lift the little round tub of water up to the kitchen sink and over the edge.

"Thank you," said Clara. "Ah, that's better." She stood down on her foot, on top of a terry cloth towel. "There's nothing like Epsom Salts, is there?"

"No indeed," answered Rose. "So what do you think?" she asked. "Did you find out where she went last night?"

"If you mean Bernice, the answer is no, I didn't."

"Well," began Rose, "according to Sam Jaworski down at the bakery, he heard from his son, who heard from a reliable source, that she was in Philadelphia again!"

"To see Katie."

"Well. . .yes, I guess that's what she would say."

Clara said nothing but put away the tub, closed up the cabinet and washed her hands. "Tea?"

"Yes, please," said Rose rising. "Don't you find that strange? That two weekends in a row—or is it 3, I lose track, she goes out on a Friday night to see her aunt, in Philadelphia?"

"All I can say, Rose, is that Kate is a lucky woman to have inspired such interest and even loyalty in so young a girl. I congratulate her."

Rose was stumped. Temporarily. Yes, that certainly was something to be grateful for, she reasoned. But, no, simply not plausible.

"Well, I, too, congratulate her," she said. "That is if indeed it's where she's been going."

Clara handed her friend a Gorham tea cup and saucer, roses and ribbons swirled in the design in Clara's delicate but sturdy hand. "You're so suspicious, Rose," she said and took a seat. "I'm not going to give you any of my ginger cake."

"Well I don't want it anyway," said Rose.

"Yes, you do," said Clara.

"Well anyway, I think you're being stubborn is all," said Rose. "And you sure have changed *your* tune."

"Oh," sighed Clara, handing her friend a plate of ginger cake. "It's just so upsetting—I don't know if I really want to know."

Rose hesitated, but then went on boldly. "Don't you remember that little Joan Foster *also* packed a suitcase and left town last weekend? Where do you think she was off to? Also Aunt Kate's? I don't think so," she finished slyly.

"Well they certainly didn't go away together," said Clara.

"Oh of course not. What would be the point of that? No, I think they met up somewhere else, maybe with some men. . ." Her voice trailed off and her whole manner seemed to brighten. "Perhaps the two of them secretly met with some men, to elope!" she finished triumphantly.

"Well Rose, that hypothesis might carry more weight if it weren't for the fact that they are both back home now and both unmarried."

"Hmm. . ." was all she said.

"Look at that pile of chicken!" cried Helen as she came into the kitchen. "And boy does it smell good in here!"

"That ought to feed a hungry sailor or two," said Annie taking off her apron.

"What are you wearing tonight?" Joan asked.

"Well that's changing the subject," Bernice laughed. "I thought I was the one who did that kind of thing."

Annie and Helen laughed.

"What?" asked Joan, truly confused. "Oh, I guess you could say I was a little preoccupied."

"Oh?" said Helen. "With what?"

"Or who?" said Annie.

"Whom," corrected Bernice.

Three pairs of eyebrows raised. "Bernice?" said Helen. "Are you majoring in English this month?"

"It probably sounds really funny," Bernice confessed, "but I can't stand poor English. I mean I like Annie's bad English—"

"*What!*" said Annie.

"I mean when you get all downtowny and all. But--"

"*Town*" Annie said through gritted teeth, "Down*town*."

"Yeah," Bernice when on, "but when people are speaking normally, I like them to use proper English."

"Well I think that's—" began Joan.

"So let me get this straight. It's okay for me, because I got dis downtown *handicap*," Annie said, exaggerating her accent. "But yous guys all gotta speak proper 'cause yous know better."

"Right," said Bernice as Annie scowled and Joan giggled. "So it's hard for me to keep from jumping in there and correcting you."

"For my part," Joan said, "correct away. My dad does it all the time anyway."

"You can try where I'm concerned," said Helen, "but I don't never speak bad." Everybody laughed.

"Yeah, so what do we do when *you* mess up?" Annie demanded. "Make you wear the dunce cap?"

"Sure, I could borrow one from your collection," Bernice shot back.

"I hate to interrupt," said Helen, "but we are running short on time. Let's get this chicken put away, covered and chilled, so you can get ready for the dance. I've got to find my silver polish. My sodality pin is black with tarnish."

"Come with us, Bernice," offered Joan. "We can just pick up your stuff at your house, take you back to our place and then all leave from there. Is Henry coming?"

"Nah," was all Bernice said.

Father Bertrand thanked the ladies from the
Sodality Society and the USO organizers and retired
to the rectory for the evening. He had no objection to
dances. But he didn't feel there was a place for him in
the midst of these kinds of gatherings. At 50 years of
age, he had plenty of spring left in his step and lots of
zest for life, but even as a young man, he'd never
found the same joy as others had in dances and
parties. He had always preferred one-on-one
situations; conversations with meaning and levity
where he was an active participant. He didn't really
understand it, but he accepted it, and when it came
time for events such as the one being held, he was
grateful for the participation of his parish's many
committees.

As he walked the short distance to his front door,
he was startled by the soft meow of a tiny kitten
sitting on the step. The rain earlier in the day had left
its coat muddy, and now, the wind had caked it tight
around the little creature's eyes and nose.

"Well, what do we have here?" Father asked,
stooping down to take a look. "And how in the world
did you end up here with this weather?"

He scooped up the tiny kitten and carried it
inside. The house was warm, and he set the kitten on
top of a towel next to his bathroom sink. "You won't
like a bath," he said, "but you're getting one."

To his surprise, the kitten put up very little fight
as he sponged the mud from its face and feet, and
long, lush tail. When he had finished, he discovered

that it was a black and white female kitten with long hair and blue eyes.

"I've never seen anything as pretty as you," he said as he carried her into the kitchen. "How about we start you off with some cracker crumbs and milk? My mother used to feed little strays chicken parts, but I'm afraid I'm fresh out."

The little kitten did not hesitate and before long, sat washing her tiny face and hands on the rug in front of the kitchen sink.

"You are certainly a delight," Father said. "Celestial visitor. How about if I call you Celeste?"

The kitten looked up at him as if to say, Okay, that's fine. He laughed and let her sit on his lap as he had his own dinner and read the paper.

"Look at that chicken go," said Bernice.

"Yeah," Annie agreed. "They're eating like it's their last meal."

"For some of them it might feel like it is," said Helen.

"I wonder if that's real red hair," said Joan.

The other three turned to look at her. "Hair?" asked Annie. "On the chicken? Ew! Where?"

"Ye gads, Joan," said Bernice. "That's disgusting."

Joan giggled.

"I think," said Helen, "she's talking about on that young lady's head." She indicated with a thumb over her shoulder. "The gal at the punch bowl."

"Oh," said Bernice. "You want me to pluck one and we could look at the root?"

Annie laughed. "Yeah, we'll shanghai her. You go on up alongside her, and I'll distract her while you pluck." Bernice erupted into sprays of laughter, trying alternately to control herself, and giving in to joke.

Joan felt hopeful for a moment, and then came back to her senses. Nobody was going to shanghai and pluck. "You guys are so great," Joan said. "Humor can take the sting out of almost anything."

"She's right," said Helen, turning to the table behind them to collect some of the used cups and put them into the large metal basin. "You girls are each of you a gem for the other two."

"You, too, Helen," said Annie, squeezing her arm.

"As you get older," Helen said, smiling, and looking at the floor, "you appreciate your girlfriends more and more. They mean so much, especially at times like these."

"You mean when you lose the man you wanted," said Joan, smiling sadly.

"No!" Helen came back with vigor. "Not at all! I was talking about when your husband's overseas. Listen Joan, you haven't lost anything. Old red frizz over there doesn't have him either."

Bernice began to laugh again, stomping her foot. "Oh Helen, you *are* the limit."

"No, I mean it. What did your friend Laureen tell you?"

"She said she didn't know what was happening because Bob was so busy he couldn't get in touch with Dick. Oh look, here's Margaret. Now whatever you do, don't ignore her!"

"Margaret," said Annie. "Nice to see you."

"Yes," said Margaret, as a shorter-than-she fellow struggled to catch up with her. "And this is Dominic, the baker's son. They're bringing us bread."

"Oh yeah," said Annie. "Aint my family good enough for you no more?"

"Don't get on your high horse, Annie. I'm talking about 'us,' meaning St. Benedict's. The school. You know Calabria's out of Philly supplies us."

Annie nodded but nevertheless gave the man a challenging nod.

"And this is Joan," she said, "and Bernice."

Dominic nodded at Joan, and turned to nod at Bernice. But then he stopped and raised his eyebrows just for an instant, when Bernice thrust out her hand.

"Uh, nice to *meet* you Dominic," she said, her eyes mildly panicked.

"Yeah. . ." he said, "it's nice to meet you, too."

Annie and Joan exchanged glances.

"All right, all right," said Margaret separating their hands. "You don't have to become bosom buddies. I just thought it was my obligation to introduce you. Dominic has to go. He's working tonight."

"That's a shame," said Bernice.

"Isn't it?" said Margaret, narrowing her eyes.

"Uh, Joan," Bernice continued, "Did you say Bob and Laureen didn't know where Dick was this weekend?

"Yeah," said Joan. "Unfortunately."

Bernice nudged Annie as she and Annie faced the door, while Joan faced them.

"Oh?" said Annie, starting to giggle again. "They didn't know where Dick was?"

Joan looked at her crossly. "I honestly don't see why that's funny," she said.

"You will in a minute," said Annie, indicating the far side of the hall.

Helen turned. "My stars!" she said.

Joan held her breath. "Is it him?"

Nobody answered.

"Well?" she said.

"Turn around and look for yourself, you goose," said Bernice.

Joan held her breath and turned.

And there he was, tall and gorgeous. Rich brown eyes, a shock of nearly black hair over his forehead. To Joan he looked like a movie star. The band started to play "I Don't Want to Set the World on Fire." Dick's eyes searched the room, sending a thrill to her stomach like a roller coaster ride as Joan waited breathlessly. Was he looking for her? It seemed like longer, but in only a few seconds Dick's eyes landed right on Joan's. She smiled involuntarily. He strode toward her as the singer started to sing. It was utter bliss.

Her friends discreetly crept away to the next serving table.

And then, not 10 feet from Joan, Dick was intercepted. The bottom fell out of the movie score, and at the same time, the singer's voice cracked and a soldier dropped a glass that shattered loudly. Two of the hostesses nearby ran for a broom and dustpan and collided.

"For crying out loud!" said Bernice.

"It's like a train wreck," said Annie.

"Girls, let's get Joan. She might. . . do something."

Joan was standing there with her mouth open, watching the little redhead dance around Dick, laughing and chattering like a deranged parrot. Dick was clearly caught off guard, severely knocked off course, and possibly disconcerted, but he maintained his decorum, and stood listening, nodding and smiling as one does in such situations. Joan was tempted to stomp her foot a few times and take off, head down, tearing into the little pipsqueak, but with the return of her three friends, she came back to her senses. "Oh!" she fired out. "I could just spit!"

"Well don't do *that*," said Helen. "Just. . . stay the course."

"Yeah," said Annie. "Remember what they say, 'It aint over 'til it's over.'"

Red was taking him by the hand, urging him to the dance floor. He was smiling, and raising the other hand palm up, shaking his head. But the redhead was not to be deterred, and continued her efforts relentlessly. The song played on and Dick must have felt he was losing ground, as he leaned forward, looked the little nymph in the eye and said, "Excuse me."

Bernice felt like clapping, but she satisfied herself by clapping Annie on the back.

"Let's get away from here," said Annie.

Helen nodded and they started to move away again as Dick completed his overdue journey, redhead not far behind.

But before Dick, Joan, Laureen or even Miss Redhead could say a word, Margaret stomped in and presented herself to Dick.

"Looks like we can have that dance now," she said.

"Oh, well. . . " Dick said, at once amused and grateful, "by all means."

And off they trotted to the dance floor, leaving Joan and Laureen giggling, and Miss Redhead tapping her toe and narrowing her eyes at Joan. "You planned that, didn't you?"

"I. . . I don't think I could have if I tried!" Joan said.

After a few seconds of glaring, the Redhead strutted off to the table across the room, and friends who were waiting for her there.

"Oh Joan, you've done it now!" Laureen giggled. "I don't think we've seen the last of Ruby Redhead."

They turned to watch Dick and Margaret on the floor. Margaret seemed to be counting, but Dick was smooth as ice and made them look like a couple of pros.

Joan felt a sense of peace she hadn't felt in a long time.

When Margaret's dance was over, Dick thanked her, and strolled back toward Joan and Laureen. They all found places at the table and when the waiter came around, ordered high balls.

"Do you like Coca Cola?" Dick asked Joan.

Joan thought about it. "You know, I've never been able to drink a whole Coke," she said.

"We could always share," he said, his eyes bright with humor.

"You better watch him, Joan," said Bob. "He's a sly one."

Laureen giggled. "Well if that's not the pot calling the kettle black!" she said.

"If you mean he might step on your toes on the dance floor," said Margaret, "Bob's wrong. You don't have to watch out. He's very good."

"Oh I noticed that," said Joan, and then immediately she blushed with embarrassment. "Oh! I didn't mean to say we were staring—"

"We *were* staring," Laureen said rescuing her. "We didn't want some strange man whisking Margaret away, so we were keeping an eye on you."

Margaret turned and patted Laureen's hand. "I appreciate that," she said solemnly. "I really do."

Boy, thought Joan. That Laureen can really think on her feet.

"I would, uh," Dick began, picking up the thread of the conversation, "like the opportunity to prove myself." He stood and offered his hand to Joan. Turning to Laureen and winking, he said, "We'll dance close by so you can keep an eye on me."

"I will," said Laureen, playing the game.

"And so will I," said Margaret.

Bob chuckled and put an arm around his girl.

Joan and Dick glided off to the floor, the music in Joan's heart learning a whole new rhythm.

Chapter Seven

The City Diner stood halfway between Abottsville and Atlantic City, regal in its neon majesty.

"Let's get a booth on the bay side," said Joan, breathless with excitement. "How many are we?"

"Six," said Annie, "if you count Bernice."

"Eight if you count Annie," rejoined Bernice.

"I don't get it," said Laureen to Joan.

"They're always picking at each other, don't worry about it," giggled Joan.
Bob and Dick were deep in conversation when the ladies returned from the powder room.

"There they are," said Dick. "Even lovelier than before."

"He means me," said Annie. "Don't you, Dick?"

"Oh shut up Annie," said Bernice. "Everybody knows he's talking about. . . me."

Everyone laughed as Joan took a seat on the booth next to Dick, looking shyly at the menu. Laureen scooted in next to Bob leaving the other two to face each other.

"Is it bacon and eggs all around?" asked Dick.

"Oh not me, I'll just have coffee," said Joan.

"Just coffee? How about we split a piece of pie, Joanie," said Bernice.

"Okay, if they have any." Joan turned to check the shelves. "I don't see any." She turned to face Dick and said, "I'm very picky about my crust."

He chuckled. "You don't want it burnt," he said, "like my mother does them?"

"It's not that, but no, you're right, not overdone. But I don't like a thick crust. And I don't want it too sweet, either. A good pie crust should hold the pie together, taste good, and look nice. But it shouldn't be the feature on the pie."

"Gosh," chirped Bernice. "It's too bad Helen's not here. She loves attending home economics classes."

Joan pretended to slap her. "Well, he asked," she said.

"I agree," said Dick. "And I like plenty of filling."

"See?" said Joan to Bernice.

Bernice made a face.

"My mom doesn't do much with pies," said Annie. "But she can sure bake a mean cheesecake."

"You're not lying!" said Bernice.

"Well I want in on this dessert paradise!" cried Laureen. "Joanie, you've been holding out on me!"

"You really should get together with us, Laur," said Annie. "You would have a great time."

"Definitely," Joan said. "Don't forget—I want to exchange telephone numbers with you *tonight*."

Joan was on a cloud. Conversation hadn't come easy at first with this new man, and the first part of the night she had strived to overcome that. Yet he seemed to so easy and willing to just accept things as they developed, but was gently insistent—to her great delight—to be in her company. The fact that there may be precious few opportunities for the two of them to meet before his and Bob's departure sparked the atmosphere with both desperation and excitement. Joan longed to escape the reality of the times just then, but at the same time, realized that the intensity of her feelings rested on their very circumstances.

"So what's the story on the pie?" Dick was asking the waitress.

"It's apple tonight," she said. "Would you like some with your eggs?"
Bernice and Annie together burst out laughing.

"Hey, there's some South Jersey hospitality for you, Dick," said Annie.

"I guess I'll have it separate, thank you," he said, chuckling. "But bring some for my girl, here."

Joan caught her breath, thrilled. The other three girls gave her the look. Her heart suddenly grew warm with a deep sentiment of belonging.

"Yeah," said Bernice heartily, "bring his girl a piece of that pie." She gave Joan a knowing look.

"What?" Dick asked, feigning mild confusion.
Joan unintentionally moved just a little closer to him.

Bob and Laureen shared a sundae and Annie had eggs, toast, and coffee.

"This is a wonderful diner," said Dick. "We've got one at home that looks like it used to be a railroad car. Open 24 hours. All the old timers go there."

"Is it nice in Washington, D.C.?" Annie asked. "I've always wanted to go there."

"It's home to me," said Dick, "so I guess I like it. How about you, Bob?"

"Right now, if it's where Laureen is, I like it, so I guess the answer is 'no.'" He gave her a kiss on the cheek.

"Not for long," she said, smiling.

Joan found herself very happy, content to just sit and listen to the lively conversation around her. Even Annie's and Bernice's horseplay made her feel joy. But after a while, she felt she ought to try to contribute to the conversation again.

"Will you have anything else?" asked the waitress.

"Not me," said Joan and Annie at the same time, then looked at each other and laughed.

"Me neither," said Bernice.

Laureen and Bob were staring silently into each other's eyes, and Dick took advantage of the opportunity. "I'll have a banana split," he said, "and make it a double."

"Double banana split, okay," the waitress repeated and headed for the kitchen.

Joan smiled her most charming smile at him. "A double banana split!" she said. "After bacon, eggs, potatoes, toast, *and* a slice of apple pie? Where do you put it all? Do you have a third leg?"

Dick look startled, and Bob instantly came to attention.

"Uh. . .," Dick began.

"Hollow!" hissed Annie into Joan's ear.

"What?" Joan whispered, turning.

"Hollow!" Annie repeated a little more urgently. "You say, does he have a *hollow* leg."

"Oh—well what did I say?" Joan whispered back.

"You said 'third.'"

Joan could feel the entire world beginning to slide out from under her. The diner and she were becoming one mushy red hot embarrassed substance. Just when she thought she would pass out, the choked silence at the table suddenly erupted in peals of laughter coming from all directions.

"Holy cow, Joanie!" cried Bernice. "Kind of forward, aren't you?"

Joan began to feel relieved, but at the same time on the verge of tears. Annie nudged her with her shoulder, as she wiped her own eyes from laughter. Dick touched her hand and she looked up at him. His rich brown eyes were dancing with laughter, but still he struggled, trying to contain himself for her sake. Joan felt a pang of love for the second time that day. And then she started to giggle, and then to really laugh. God bless him, she thought.

The tables of folks around them wondered about the joke, but they would be left to wonder.

"Golly," Bob said to Dick, jostling him on the shoulder, "these New Jersey gals are something, huh?"

As Dick returned to his room that night, he was thoroughly captivated by the memory of Joan. He'd known only a few well, but he could not remember ever having felt such an awe for a woman. Nor could he remember ever having been so comfortable in front of one. He'd actually missed her, longed for her,

over the preceding weeks, and now that they'd met
again, he was totally hooked.

"Well, Lord," he said out loud, "Maybe the
monastery really *wasn't* for me. I was so sure that was
what You wanted me to do. But they knew, the
monsignor knew. And they were right. It looks like
You have saved this precious gift to the last. And I
could never have imagined how overwhelming and
wonderful it would feel." His emotions overcame
him in a rare moment of vulnerability. He went to his
knees to say a prayer of thanksgiving.

Outside his door in the hotel hallway, soldiers
were cutting up and horsing around, some of them
telling off color jokes, but Dick was peacefully
cocooned in what felt to him like heaven on earth.

"You're staying," said Annie as she shut the door.

"I would have even if you didn't invite me," said
Bernice.

Joan was hanging up her coat and took Bernice's
jacket. "It's definitely getting chilly out there."

"Oh you're so very casual, huh?" said Annie.

Joan said nothing but could not keep from smiling
as she got out some cupcakes from her packed bag of
party leftovers. Then she turned on the kettle. "I'm
so glad he came."

"You know, Joan, he really is a nice guy."

"I know it."

"He's a gentleman. He's got some class. You
should be proud."

"I don't know about proud," said Joan. "After all, he's not mine yet—"

"Oh he will be," piped in Bernice from across the room. "Geeze, this scapular," she said trying to untangle if from her string of pearls.

"So you're wearing it again," said Annie. "That's nice to see."

"Hey you don't have a corner on the market of goodness," said Bernice.
Joan laughed. "Yeah, Annie, other people are good, too, you know."

"Well, I apologize," Annie said, bowing in an exaggerated fashion to Bernice. "I did not mean to imply anything."

"Oh yes you did," said Bernice. "You meant it's a good thing since I'm such a little cut up."

"I'm just glad you're wearing it," said Annie.

"Yeah, well, I'm glad you're wearing yours, too," said Bernice. "And you, too, Joan."

Joan instinctively grasped the little felt and fabric rectangle with the image of the Blessed Mother on it that hung on a brown cord around her neck. "I don't ever want to be without it," she said. "I wonder if Dick wears one. I didn't see it."

"Well, you wouldn't," said Annie. "He had on a suit."

"Does Sylvester?" Bernice asked.

"If he does, I haven't noticed it," Annie said. "I've never wondered that before. I should ask him in my next letter."

"Yeah. Tell him we're taking a survey," Bernice said. "But back to you, Joan, how about this man coming all the way up here for just a local dance? And Bob said they had roomed together, got a place at the last minute on a Friday night. He must really care for you."

Before Joan could break from her pleasant reverie, Annie jumped in.

"Yeah—Friday night. How about that, Bernice?"

Bernice turned to tuck the sheet into the couch pillows. "What are you talking about?"

"It's Friday night."

"Yeah and tomorrow's Saturday. You're getting good, Annie. Next, work on the months of the year."

"I mean your regular date with your 'aunt,'" she said emphasizing the word, "in Philly. How come you're here?"

Joan grabbed the kettle off the stove as it started to whistle because she wanted to hear Bernice's answer.

"…break," said Bernice.

"What?" Annie said. "Speak up."

"Oh, here we go, Miss Downtown. Do you want I should get you a note, too?" Bernice said faking Annie's accent.

Joan burst out laughing.

"Yeah, yeah, quit stalling," said Annie.

"I said I'm giving her a break," Bernice said, and then softly to herself, "at least that's what I should have said."

Annie and Joan exchanged glances.

"I don't know about this," Annie said suspiciously.

Joan shook her head furtively at Annie. "Okay, ladies, tea time."

"I can't eat another thing!" said Bernice. "But I will."

Next morning, as a definite chill set in the air, Helen slipped on her car coat and hiked around the block to Annie and Joan's. To her surprise and delight, she found Bernice there as well.

"What a nice surprise to see all of you this morning," Helen said. "Our little craft group gets a second day this week."

"Wasn't it a great dance, Helen?" said Joan, her eyes dancing.

"It certainly was," said Helen. "At the end, not only did we break even on the tickets, but the cake and coffee table got so many donations, they're talking about doing another one in November. I was thrilled. I think it's the absolute best thing for these fellows."

"I think it's the absolute best thing for Joan," said Bernice plopping down beside Helen. She giggled, winking at Annie.

"Yes, it's good for Joan," said Annie. "It gives her a chance to learn how to make better fried chicken."

"Hey!" said Joan. "My chicken's just fine, thank you very much."

"I think they're having fun with you," said Helen. "Tell me, did you have a nice time at the diner?"

"It was terrific," said Joan, smiling.

"I think Dick is top notch," said Annie.

"I heard from one of the ladies that he had only recently become a member of the Catholic Men's Social," said Helen. "But he seems so comfortable, it made me wonder."

"We didn't really do too much discussing of stuff like that," Joan said. "Seriously, gals, you know what it's like when you just have this feeling and you don't even think about all the rest of the world? It was like that. We were just in a cloud."

"I remember those days," said Helen. She was silent for a moment, and then got a little misty and shifted through her pockets for her handkerchief. Annie felt sudden alarm. "Has something happened?"

"No, no, not that I know of," said Helen wiping her eyes. "But I just have a feeling. . ."

Annie was tense. She'd not heard from Sylvester either in several days, which was unusual. "What do you mean, have a feeling? Did he say something in his last letter?"

"His last letter was different, Annie," Helen said, pausing to remember it in her mind. "I can't quote from it or put my finger on the exact words, but something about it was different."

"Kind of like something was going to happen?" Annie asked.

Helen looked up sharply. "Why do you ask that?"

"Because that's the feeling I got from Sylvester's last letter. Ever since he left for Europe, I've been on edge, but that letter..."

The two women stared at each other for a moment.

"And ever since they moved Harry from Africa, I've had this feeling, a kind of uncertainty."

"He's Army, isn't he, Helen?" Joan asked.

"Yes, but from what he could tell me, his unit and several others in the maintenance were going to be supporting another group, the Strategic something or other."

"Northwest Africa Strategic Air Force?" Annie asked.

"Yes! How on earth did you know?"

"They're traveling in Cargo planes, sort of like in the bellies of them, like sacks of flour. I read it in one of letters my mother got from Uncle Paulie. It made me wonder because Sylvester is in the Navy, but I have never known where he is except that I'm pretty sure he's helping with his linguistic ability, in Italian. Uncle Paulie's supposed to be doing the same thing but yet he's in the Army."

"I didn't know they mixed them all up like that," said Joan.

"Oh yes," said Helen. "If you're in linguistics, or maintenance for that matter, you can end up anywhere, even under English or French commanders."

Annie felt suddenly morose. "Oh Helen. We have no idea where they are, do we?"

Helen put an arm around her and gave her a squeeze. "That's why we've got to keep up our prayers, keeping vigilant. Don't let a day go by, not even a meal, without offering a prayer or making a sacrifice for them. It's so important."

Annie nodded, her eyes closed.

Joan put her arm around Bernice. "Gosh you guys, we're here for you, too, you know that."

"You can count on us," said Bernice. "We are all in this together. Nobody's alone in any part of it. And remember, 'I am always with you, even unto the ends of the world.' Don't forget that."

Annie and Joan exchanged glances. "Wow, Bernice," was all Annie said.

"Bernice knows just the right thing to say," said Helen smiling. "Thanks, Honey. That quotation keeps everything in perspective."

Chapter Eight

On September 9, 1943, as Eleanor Roosevelt was stepping off the plane in Queensland, Australia, and B-26 Bombers were hitting German-held targets in Scanzano, Jonico, Italy, individual Italian citizens were meeting secretly to organize a human blockade of German munitions in their native Napoli. Having lost some of their bravest leaders, the Italian opposition was sobered, but not cowed by the Nazis, and continued to carefully construct plans in tiny compartments of well-concealed attics.

Unlike the Nazis' well-penetrated presence in France, their position in Italy was sketchy. They remained largely in the dark about the captive city of Napoli, where citizens spoke little and revealed less to their Nazi captors. Surprised and frustrated by the state of affairs, the Germans had tried strong-arm tactics and threats of deportation to slave camps. They experienced very little success even then, and remained relatively ignorant of the goings on in their recently acquired spoils.

In a tiny farmhouse, south of the city proper, where not a single Mussolini sympathizer could be found, two Americans sat eating; one tall and dark, in his middle twenties, and one shorter and much older.

"I was sure I'd be in the thick of things by now, what is it, the 15th?" said the tall one.

"September 12. Just be glad you're not," said the older one. "I guarantee, I never had anything this delicious in my last war. What do they call this again?"

"It's calamari. Really good for you, too."

"You on tonight?"

"Nope," said the tall one. "My orders are continue to stay with Constanzi and lay low 'til needed. I'm bored to death."

The shorter older fellow laughed. "Good!"

Three miles away, a group was just breaking up, silently returning to their homes for the mid-day. The plan was set. Whatever would happen, would happen. The Napoladans would not stand for the Nazi imposition. Many were fired up by vendetta, considering themselves avenging angels, and wore the sign of an angel inside the right lapel. Others were simply in support of the angels and against the Nazis. They formed a tight, well-run, well-organized fighting faction, disguised by a loose, laughing, devil-may-care attitude.

Rose and Clara walked down 23rd Street on a mission to deliver a basket of flowers at St. Benedict's.

"If I had known it was going to be this chilly," said Clara, "I would have let Pauline drive us."

"Well did she offer?"

"No, Rose, but if I had asked her, I'm sure she would have."

"Well, she saw you walking by," said Rose.

"What is your point?"

"My point is, Clara, that we ought not to impose on our children. It makes us unwanted."

"You haven't got any children."

"Well."

"If you don't have any—"

"What is that?" said Rose, circling back to the rectory side of the church. "It sounds like a man singing."

Father Bertrand had been out to check the mail while his parishioners were laying the flowers in the church. He'd let his little Celeste outside to visit with nature while he made the short walk to his mailbox and back. Just as the ladies were journeying down the steps of the church, Father was gathering up his kitten, who very agreeably snuggled in his arms.

"You are something!" said the happy priest. "I have never had a kitten before, but if I had known how pleasant you all could be, I most certainly would have before now. Let's go inside and see what there is to eat!" At that, he opened the door and began to sing, making up a set of lyrics to "Kitten on the Keys," in his rich baritone voice. "You're my Kitty on the, Kitty on the, Kitty on the keys!"

"It *is* a man singing," said Clara. "It's Father Bertrand!"

Rose cocked her head. "What's he saying? It sounds like 'Kitty.'"

Clara nodded, her eyes wide. "He's singing to a woman!"

Rose's mouth fell open. "No!"

"Well," said Clara, resolutely, and turning hard on her heel. "Let's go. It's not our business."

"But—"

"Come *on*, Rose!"

The two old ladies made a quick exit in silence, as Father Bertrand continued on in the background, "Kitty, Kitty, Kitty, my sweet Kitten on the Keys!"

Twelve beautiful shell creations sat on the marble shelf in Helen's living room. A tall rectangularly shaped one, a collection of various colors and sizes had been arranged so as to reflect a day of very colorful snow against a ribbon-covered cardboard background. Helen paused on her way to the kitchen and smiled. She picked it up and studied it. The hat, the boot, and her roses, and the rest were all very pretty and definitely purchase-worthy, as Annie would say. But Bernice's creation was not just different, it somehow seemed inspired, uplifting. Helen wondered how the other girls would react.

"Helen?" Joan called from the door.

"Come on in, Honey," Helen said. "Take off your jacket and join me for a cup of tea while we wait for the others."

"Oh look at all these pretty things!" said Joan, as she laid down her jacket. "We've done some good work. And hey, is this what Bernice did?"

"Yes. Isn't that something?"

"Golly," said Joan. She picked up the little card and studied it. "I never would have thought of doing anything like that with it. It's like a painting, isn't it?"

"I didn't think of that way, but you're right. It is like a painting. And I agree. It is very inspired."

"Could it be that Bernice has finally found a craft she can really do?" Joan said with enthusiasm.

Helen gave her arm a squeeze. "You're such a good friend," she said. "I have to say, I feel it, too. Bernice is a good sport, but she does feel it when she's not able to do some of the things we can. And here she's taken what we were doing and somehow maybe even elevated it."

At meeting's end, the girls had chocked up another four shell creations for sale at the Bazaar.

"We're moving now," said Annie.

"Nothing's going to stop us now!" Bernice chimed in.

"Yeah, I really like what you're doing," said Annie. "It's different and really creative."

"Oh go on, Annie," said Bernice, embarrassed.

"I mean it."

"So do I," said Joan.

"And me," said Helen. "I think you've really got something there. Maybe you could show us how to do it."

Bernice laughed. "Okay, now I *know* you're joking! When is the bazaar, anyway?"

"It's the 8th, isn't it, Helen?" Annie said.

Helen nodded. "Yep. December 8th. We're going to have a very busy season, it looks like, with Midnight Mass, the Christmas Bazaar, and now possibly the Thanksgiving Dance. Hey, speaking of which, Joan, what do you hear from Dick?"

"I got the nicest letter," she said smiling. "He said he had a great time and loved seeing all of us again."

"Oh I love romantic letters!" Annie cooed.

"Well I wouldn't know," said Bernice.

"Oh. . . sorry, Bernice, I—"

"Hey, I'm just joking with you," she said, chuckling. "I'm actually happy for you both. And you, too, Helen. You're getting your share of love letters, I hope."

"Well, they're probably not quite the same tone as Joan's and Annie's," Helen said. "But yes, I guess you could say I'm getting my share, although I would rather have Harry home, just the same. And they have been few and far between lately. . . "

"Maybe there'll be something in the afternoon post," Joan said.

"And if not, it's not like we don't have enough to keep us busy," said Annie. "Even with the shop open less this month, I'm still busy with something or other all day."

"And it's just going to get busier—you're right. It's a blessing," Helen said. "I guess we better get cleaned up."

"Keep us posted on the plans for a Thanksgiving Dance, won't you, Helen? As soon as you hear anything?" said Joan.

"Oh don't you worry, I sure will!"

Just as the three girls put on their coats, a knock came at the door.

"Oh, maybe that's your letter," said Bernice. "Does your mailman knock?"

Before she could answer, in came Rose Parlavita and Clara Centonze.

"Hi Grandma," said Bernice. "What brings you here? Hi Mrs. Parlavita."

"Hello girls. We had something to discuss with Mrs. Ashenbach," said Clara.

"Sure thing, Mrs. St. John," said Annie. "We gals are just heading out. Bernice, can I give you a lift?"

After they'd dropped Bernice off, Joan suggested they stop by the A&P for a couple of things. "Do you have the ration book?"

"Yes, I do," Annie said. "And we're in good shape."

Bernice relished the opportunity to be home alone. She loved her mother and her grandmother, and even her grandmother's next door neighbor, but there was nothing like solitude. Especially now. Every day she felt stronger and more certain and enormously happy.

In her bedroom was a picture of Henry. She couldn't help smiling as she picked up it, remembering their last meeting. "Well gee whiz, Bernice," he'd said, his eyes wide, "No, I'm not mad. How could I be? We've known each other almost our whole lives. I could never be mad at you." She wondered when he would be called up. It was certain he would be. He had enlisted as soon as they'd graduated last spring. She would worry about him. She knew that. No matter what happened in her life.

She checked the clock and saw she still had five minutes before vespers. "I bet I'll be the only one from our group who shows up today!" she laughed. She grabbed her coat and hat, and overnight bag, and slipped out the door.

As Bernice approached the steps to St. Benedict's Church, she spotted Laureen coming from the opposite direction. "Laureen," she said, "How ya doing?"

"Hi Bernice," said Laureen. "I don't usually make it to vespers but I had a shaky feeling today that Bob might just get shipped out soon and I thought it couldn't hurt."

"I love this service," said Bernice. "It's usually one of the quietest, too. Me and the girls go on the first one of the month, but not every week. So you think Bob will be going overseas?"

"Oh, I'm pretty sure he will. And Dick, too, of course. It's torture not knowing. Some of the girls are going ahead and getting married before the men go, but I want to have a regular wedding, not a rush-rush job. And one where we can have a nice reception," she added. "It's not much fun to have a party and offer nothing good to eat!"

Bernice burst out laughing, but then quickly covered her mouth as they opened the door to the church. "That's for sure!" she whispered. "Have a nice service. I want to sit in the choir loft."

"Good to see you, Bernice!" Laureen whispered back.

From the choir loft, up above the two rows of pews, Bernice could see the whole church, except the last few rows in the back. The view was always comforting, especially as the war seemed to just get worse and worse. From up above, she could see the stained-glass windows that spanned from front to back on both sides of the church. She saw the life-sized white marble statue of St. Benedict, and the candles flickering in front of the statue of the Blessed Mother. Her heart went out to all the mothers and sweethearts who had lit those candles for their soldiers in combat. But amidst all of the longing and fear, folks found solace here, as she always had, and most especially up in the loft, where she found it peaceful with only the organist and their small weekday choir present.

"You'll be singing with us next week, right?" whispered Bitsy, the organist and choir leader, as she turned a page.

"If you really want me," said Bernice.

Bitsy winked. She turned and whispered to the choir, "All right ladies, Ave Verum Corpus."

The choir began the rich strains of the beloved Mozart with Latin stanzas. As the hymn took shape, Bernice imagined she could see angels floating above them.

"Well, there are the three basic conflicts," said Joan as Annie pulled onto the highway. "You've got man against man, man against nature, and then man against himself."

"Okay."

"So in every situation, it's got to be one of those three."

"Well, war, this war, is definitely man against man, then," said Annie.

"Yes, but it turns into the other two, eventually."

"Uh. . ."

"Well, what happens over winter? Sure they're fighting," Annie said. "But remember that newsreel, the snow?"

"Oh, I see what you mean. But how does the man against himself come into it?"

"I don't really know for sure, but probably later, hopefully, the bad men will feel that. How could they have done such a thing, they'll think."

"Oh Joan, I doubt it. I really do."

"I know it sounds pretty farfetched."

"Hitler? Mussolini? Certainly not that Nipponese man."

"Do you think they really believe they're doing the right thing?"

"I don't think they think like we do. I don't think right and wrong even enter into the picture. Let me put it this way; if they lose, they're wrong. If they win, they're right. That's how they see it."

Joan sighed. "I guess a war was inevitable then."

Annie nodded. "Yeah."

The miles rolled by quietly for a while with fewer cars on the road than Annie remembered on her last journey to North Jersey. "It's nice of you coming with me. I know Mom and Pop appreciate it."

"I'm happy to do it! I don't know how you got enough rations to fill up this big tank, but it's always the bus for me, and I like to travel. So this is extra nice."

"Well, if this is travel, you are easy to please."

The girls laughed. But there was a restlessness in the laughter, and then in the silence.

After a while, Joan said, "What do you think Helen meant about being uneasy? You know, her letter from Harry?"

Annie shook her head. "I have the same feeling. Kind of an anticipation, you know? Like a nervous—yeah, that's it, nervousness. Anyway, that was how I felt after I read Sylvester's letter, not that *he* was uneasy. It was me, I felt that way after I read it. Know what I mean?"

"I wonder if something big is going to happen."

"Well that's just it, Joanie. We don't know nothin' 'til it's done, 'til it's happened, the results are in, and they're mopping it *aawl* up!" Annie sighed.

Joan grabbed her hand. Annie was so easy to read these days; her accent flowed like black coffee when she was upset.

"Even now," Annie continued, "Sylvester could be, could be . . . " her voice trailed off as she tried to get ahold of her emotions.

"Oh no, Annie. Try not to think that way. If something had gone wrong, you would know. You would feel it."

Annie wrinkled her brow. "Do you really think so?"

"I know it. Once you're that close, that in love with a man, you know when something's affecting him."

"I hope you're right."

"Let's talk about something else. Let's talk about Bernice!" she giggled.

"I can't believe she went to vespers and we didn't!" Annie said. "What a gal."

"Well we'll *all* be going this Friday, so she won't have anything on us."

"Phooey, Joanie, it's not a competition."

Joan looked out the window.

"Hey and what do you think of that beautiful card she made out of shells? I think she's got something there," said Annie.

"You're right. I really did like that. I guess I'm just . . ."

"Jealous?" teased Annie.

"Oh a little, I guess. But also, confused, or curious or something. What is going on with her? How did she suddenly start taking Friday night classes? And why all the way in Philadelphia? Why not here somewhere?"

"I guess they don't have them in Abbotsville. What was it in, anyway?"

"I don't think she ever said. Or maybe yes, I can't remember."

Annie was quiet for a moment. "You know, Joan, I think she's going through something. I don't see her with Henry anymore. She never talks about him, you notice. She may just have found herself another fella and she wants to keep it quiet for a while. You know what I mean?"

"Yeah. You might be right. I was thinking along the same lines."

"I'm going to pass this guy. He must be doing 20."

"But then she went and joined the choir. I mean, if she's got a fellow in Philly—"

"Hey, that sounds like a song—I got myself a fella in Philly," Annie sang out, as she maneuvered her car around the slow moving DeSoto.

Joan laughed. "We agreed not to talk about that, didn't we?"

"Yes," Annie said nodding. "We agreed to keep our nasal passages out of it."

"Gotcha."

"But we can talk about our guys," said Annie smiling. "I don't know about you, but I want children. Lots of them. Right away."

"Oh golly, me, too," said Joan. "I want at least two boys and two girls."

"Hey, me too!" Annie laughed. "What do you want to call them?"

"I like Bernadette and Veronica for the girls," said Joan. "I'm not sure about the boys. What about you?"

"I want one of them to be called Mary," said Annie. "At least one Mary, and maybe Elizabeth."

"Oh that's nice. I want their middle names to be Mary. Or the French, Marie."

"That's nice, Joanie! Veronica Marie. Oh I like that! Maybe I'll steal it."

"There'll be a lot of confusion between our two homes if you do!" Joan laughed. "There can't be too many Marys though. Not in this world."

"Yes. That is one hundred percent true."

"Speaking of which, I brought my rosary."

"Good. Mine's in my pocket. When we get there," Annie said, "I'm having a whole one of those sausages to myself, and you can, too. It's the least they can do for us, driving all the way up here for it."

Joan laughed. "Hey, any time the truck is out of commission, count me in on this errand!"

"You know it. Do you want to say the Joyful Mysteries?"

"Sure. You lead."

Chapter Nine

"Hey there Captain!" called a tall, handsome, and hobbling Navy man. "Nice to see a buddy!"

"So you went and took one in the leg, did you?" Harry said. "How in the hell did that happen? You were supposed to be behind the lines—safe and sound Sly, remember?"

"Yeah, I got switched to recon for a while. At my own request. I couldn't stand sitting around. When you left on that mission, I guess I'd just had it, sitting around feasting and comfy while so many of the guys are really suffering. So I put in for recon and Captain Freda okay'd me right away. After training, I had one successful mission, ferreted out a pair of snipers over that bakery there, or what used to be one. Then 3 nights ago, whammo. They saw me coming, I guess. But my partner got'em. That's three snipes between the 2 of us. He's all right, I guess he's a better shot. It'll be something interrogating the same guys we hit!"

"They were locals?"

"No, Cap says they were part of something that came over with the last wave of Germans, but you never really know."

"I heard that!" Harry looked around. "Not so bad for a hospital, Sly," he said. "In Africa they were 12 to a room, tiny rooms, crammed in there like packed sardines. This is paradise in comparison."

"Yeah. I lead a charmed life." Sylvester chuckled. Then he shook his head and sat at one of the little tables and rested his injured leg on one of the wood stools at the table. Harry sat down and pretended to be signaling for a waitress.

"Couple of beers here, please?" he said to the wall.

Sylvester laughed again.

"It don't hurt when you laugh, does it?" Harry asked.

"No! Keep 'em coming." But then he fell serious. "I still can't believe what you did, Harry. That whole town is alive today, kids, mothers with babies, everybody, because of you."

"Not just me," Harry said quietly, looking down.

"God rest his soul. Pete was the best," said Sylvester. "But without you carrying the ball after that, rounding up them Gerrys," he shook his head. "I still don't know how you knew they were in that store. I guess that comes with experience, huh."

"Yeah, that and having a bunch of ears to the ground. Don't forget, Pete was one of twelve guys just living amongst all of them. I knew if it wasn't in the restaurant on the cliff there, it had to be somewhere inside that store. I'm glad I guessed right. I'm just sorry Pete didn't make it through. He went down early. That'll be a sad letter his wife gets when they release it. But we have to keep on, Sylvester. It's not just Naples. They're pushing hard these next few months. Clark and Montgomery both—some folks are saying Clark thinks he's in charge, but I'll tell you, boy, he sure knows his stuff. I'll give him that.

So we gotta both take this bit of time to get our strength and recover. And this is a good place to do it."

They were silent for a moment. The two men sat in a small but open room, where despite its being the 10th of October, chrysanthemums still bloomed in pots at the base of open windows. Several other wounded and visiting soldiers sat in bunches around the room, most ambulatory with healing injuries like Sylvester's.

The air was warm and breezy, but the scent of the German gunfire still hung in the air, even though it had been the better part of two weeks since they'd been routed out.

A tall raggedy boy of about ten years, dressed in a red shirt and blue and white short pants and a much shorter one about the same age wearing dark clothes and a red hat stood at the door, hoping to be sent on errands, their eyes dark, large, and shining with hope. Italian and English nurses were making the rounds with carts of both medications and tea.

"Hey let's hope they don't get those mixed up!" said Sylvester, pointing to the carts.

Harry smiled. "So when are you getting out?"

"I'm supposed to be out today," he said, gesturing over toward a door. "If they come around and sign me out."

"Good. Good news," said Harry.

"You said that like you have a reason," said Sylvester. "What's up?"

"You're right. They're moving three small units, and I'm talking eight to ten men each, to outposts, captured territories, where there will be code and messenger, like me, language assistants, like you, backup patrols, and recon. I'm second in command of one of them, and I requested you."

"Hey, we'll be working together again! Good show, Harry."

"You're going to have to call me Captain in front of the brass," Harry laughed. "It'll be a different kind of place, but interesting, I think."

"Oh yeah, where are we going?"

"It's still smoking from Allied fire," Harry said, "but before the Germans got a hold of it, it was a beautiful little island. The buzz is that the Fifth is going to cross the Volturno. I think if we give it a good honest try, we'll make it. The Allies are on a roll now. But naturally there will be casualties and prisoners to deal with. We'll be visiting with Italian prisoners brought over for questioning. I use the word *visiting* broadly."

"Gotcha."

"It's called Pantelleria."

"It seems like all we ever do is make crafts," said Annie forlornly. "Do you think there will even be anyone to buy them? Who's going to care about this stuff now, with all this going on?"

"Aw come on Annie," Bernice said, punching her in the arm without much thrust. "Your little friend is just fine. If he weren't, you would know by now. Joanie, hand me the red center ones, would you?"

Joan stood and passed Bernice the shells and looked at Annie. "I'm sorry," she said quietly. "It has to be just awful waiting to hear from the man you love." Her voice broke on the last word and she crumpled into a sobbing heap, her face in her hands.

Annie, Helen, and Bernice all looked at each other in shock.

"Oh honey," said Helen. "What is it? What's happened?"

"Yeah, Joanie, what's going on?" Annie said, rushing to her side.

"I just had a call, just this morning, from Laureen," Joan said, sniffing and coughing. "Bob and Dick's company ships out December 7th. December 7th! Talk about a bad omen." And she started to cry again.

"Oh boy, and the day before the bazaar," said Bernice, giving her a hug. "Oh you poor thing."

"Did she tell you where they were going?" Helen asked.

"No," said Joan. "She didn't know. I don't think *they* even knew."

Annie looked at Helen. "They're not telling anybody anything anymore."

"They do seem to have become very secretive lately," Helen agreed. "He's not in security, is he? Any kind of secret or spy duty that you know of?"

"Oh, she wouldn't know if he was," said Annie.

"I think they can tell you if they are," said Helen. "But they just can't tell you what they're doing. At least that's my understanding of it."

Joan sat up and wiped her nose and dabbed at her eyes. "I'm sorry gals," she said. "You are all going through the same thing. This is no different."

"No, but it's so new to you, Honey," said Helen putting an arm around her. "And it's not the nicest day to be traveling, either."

"All I know," Joan said, nodding, "is that Bob is still in the Air Corps, and their two units are shipping out together. The Air Corps. Poor Laureen. That's so scary."

No one said anything. The bombardiers were known to pass through the sky with very little trouble, being escorted by so many fighters and recon craft, but there were very few who qualified for that duty and Bob was not in that squadron. In fact, no one knew what he had trained for other than generally the Air Corps.

"Well," Bernice ventured, "maybe he'll be in the training sector, and never even have to leave the country. Did you ever think of that?"

"But Laureen said 'ship out.' Doesn't that mean go out of the country?"

"Not necessarily," Helen said. "Shipping out could me you're going to Pennsylvania."

Everyone laughed. Helen turned to the buffet behind her and brought around Annie's cheesecake. "That would be a treat," she said chuckling.

"Or Atlantic City," Bernice added.

"Wouldn't that be nice?" said Joan, smiling at Bernice. She stood up and set out the tea cups. "Sorry I got here so late, Helen. I missed helping you set up today."

Helen gestured to Joan to forget it.

"There are hundreds of bases," Annie went on. "Bernice is right. They don't have one in Atlantic City, but there's always Fort Dix. He could be there."

"The main thing is, don't fret until you know where he is. And don't fret then, either," giggled Helen. "It doesn't do anybody any good, most of all you."

"You're right," said Joan.

"You're darn right she's right," said Bernice. "And don't forget, the 7th may be an ugly day in history, but the 8th is the Feast of the Immaculate Conception. That's a great day to be arriving somewhere."

"Bernice, you are inspired! All right, then. And you and I will stop all this worrying, too. We don't know 'til we know," said Annie, looking at Helen. "We're all acting like a bunch of ninnies. Guinea I might be, but ninny, no."

Bernice laughed. "Annie, you're too much!"

"I like your advice, Annie. To be honest, I've spent my share of soggy hours when no one's around. And it makes no sense. As you say, we don't know 'til we know. Now let's have some cake and then get to work!"

By 3:00, the four were at St. Benedict's, listening to the choir. Back on the shelf at Helen's house sat many new beautiful brooches, or *pins*, as Helen referred to them, and one enormous bird-like character Bernice had made. Helen thought of it and smiled. She knew Bernice had intentionally created a mess just to keep the other girls' spirits up and she was so grateful. The girls would need a lot of Bernice moments to stay in good spirits during the next few years, or longer, as things looked now.

Back at home, later that night as Helen waited for her vegetable and cheese casserole to warm through, she sustered through her collection of fabric and fabric scraps.

It was getting dark earlier, and she'd had to draw the curtains even before she and the girls had left that afternoon for vespers. But the November air was crisp and pleasant and she let in a little through an upstairs window. Someone down the street had a fire going. Helen wasn't sure if that complied with the blackout regulations for coastal towns, but she was grateful for the lovely scent wafting through the air. She breathed it in and thought of Harry, strong and broad-shouldered, stirring up a campfire during their honeymoon.

He was such an outdoorsman. When her parents had learned that they were camping out for their honeymoon, they were incensed, but Helen went along with it. If Harry wants it, she'd figured, there must be a good reason.

And oh, she thought lovingly, there certainly had been. She could still remember waking up to the sound of mountain bluebirds in the Virginia wilds, and actually smelling wildflowers, ones she'd really only seen before in books and never bothered to hunt down in her own hometown of Terre Haute, Indiana.

And of course, there, too, was the man she loved. He'd even managed to shave in the wilderness! She laughed out loud.

She wished he could be there for their upcoming bazaar, and see her pretty hostess dress, which she had yet to make. She would make it as if he were going to be there to see it. She'd use the colors he liked and the pinafore type ruffles that he thought so feminine. She'd suggest to the girls that they do the same. Make their dresses in honor of their men. The thought made her feel warm inside. Sometimes at night, and especially with the fire smoke in the air that night, Helen felt a hollow longing, and lost, alone and terribly sad. But just as she was about to give in to a good old-fashioned cry, she remembered the mailbox.

"I never checked it today!" she said out loud. And she dashed downstairs to find a full mailbox, containing most of the usual things, and then, there it was—a letter from Harry!

She quickly shut the door and stepped inside, put the other stuff on the hall table and went to the kitchen to have a cup of tea and a nice leisurely read. It felt cozy in their kitchen, alive, as if Harry himself had actually come home. The kettle began to sing, and just as she got out a cup and saucer, a knock came at the door.

"Oh, for heaven's sakes!"

She went to the door and opened it.

"Hello, Mrs. Ashenbach. I'm sorry to barge in during dinner hour and all, but I just had to see you," said Mrs. St. John.

Helen smiled and stuffed the envelope quickly into her front pocket.

"Hello, Mrs. St. John," said Helen. "Won't you come in? I was just about to read—uh, have a cup of tea. Will you join me?"

"What? No coffee today?" said Mrs. John, as she bustled directly toward the kitchen.

"Uh, no, I guess I've not gotten my share yet this month. I—"

"Ration," said Mrs. St. John, taking a seat where Helen had set her own place. "Might as well call a spade a spade. We get *rations*."

"True enough," said Helen cheerfully. "So how are you doing these days?" She turned to get another teacup.

"Not so great," said Mrs. St. John, shortly. "And I think you know why."

Helen stopped and turned. "What? I mean what did you say?"

Mrs. St. John leaned forward scowling, tapping the table with one hand as she raised her cup for some water from the pot with the other. "My mother's been sharing information with you, hasn't she? I'll have cream."

"Why, whatever gave you that idea?" Helen asked.

"Rose said so," said Mrs. St. John. "My nosey neighbor who gets in everyone's business."

Helen turned away from her to shut off the fire under the teapot. "Well if that's not the pot calling the kettle black," she said under breath.

"What?" said Mrs. St. John sharply.

"Oh, I said, 'let me just turn off this kettle,'" said Helen, thinking, oh gosh, now I have to confess that lie. She poured Mrs. St. John's cup and began to pour her own.

"A little more, please," said Mrs. St. John. "Rose says that you entertained my mother and her while they debriefed you on the situation with Father Bertrand."

"Debriefed? Oh Mrs. St. John! It's not a criminal case! A man was heard singing a song is all."

"Singing a song to a woman," said Mrs. St. John, tapping the table again. "And a priest, who is forbidden to, to, to have women—"

"For heaven's sakes!" said Helen standing up suddenly. "You're as bad as the other two! You can't possibly think—"

"Oh yes I do think," said Mrs. John. "And if you don't, then you're closing your eyes to evil, shirking your responsibility. You're as good as condoning it, Mrs. Ashenbach!"

"And now you want to accuse me, too. You are batty!" said Helen. The night's ups and downs were taking a toll. "Isn't there enough excitement in your life? Do you have to invent some to stay happy? You're simply ridiculous!"

"Well!" said Mrs. St. John.

Helen sat down. Immediately she felt remorse for her cutting remarks. But she had no tolerance for Mrs. St. John and her excitable personality. "I'm sorry," she said, looking at her hands. "I'm just feeling the pressures, Harry gone and all."

"At least your husband is alive. Mine's long gone. It's very difficult working all the time, not knowing what's going on at home."

"I know, I know," said Helen. "But you know, Mrs. St. John, Pauline, surely you know we're not to malign or speak against the priests, especially if we don't even know anything. And if we had serious doubts, we are to write the bishop, not gossip—"

"Gossip! Is that what you think I'm doing?"

"Well. . . isn't it?"

"I'll have a cookie if you have one."

Helen was startled by the sudden change. She shouldn't have been. Mrs. St. John was famous for it. Nevertheless, she took out what remained of her Lorne Doone's and offered them. "I will be happy to inquire about the infamous Kitty," she said. "But I am certain it will come to nothing. And if I do that, I'd like you to promise that you will not spread around these ideas you and your mother and Mrs. Parlavita have. A thing like that can do more damage than good. And once it's done, it's very hard to undo."

"Yes, all right. But you sound like my daughter, suddenly Miss Goodie Two Shoes." She put a whole cookie in her mouth. "Ever since she's been out to visit my sister Kate on weekends, she acts like she's better than the rest."

Helen's eyebrows went up. She hoped Mrs. St. John had not noticed her confusion. "Your sister, Kate," she said with as little expression as she could manage.

"Yes. I think she's doing it just to annoy her mother. She knows Kate and I don't talk."

"Oh!" said Helen.

"It happens in a lot of families," Mrs. St. John said, mistaking Helen's surprise for disapproval. "Sisters don't talk, mothers and daughters don't talk." She took another cookie. "Oh I know it's not the best of examples to set for your children, but I didn't start it. And if Kate thinks I'm going to give in, she's mistaken."

"Yes, it's true," said Helen, still thinking about something entirely different. Why wouldn't Bernice have been honest with her mother? Why all the subterfuge? Yet, listening to Mrs. St. John, maybe, she thought, that wasn't such a big mystery. "Well, perhaps one day."

"Yeah. You never know. She could come to her senses."

Taking the last four cookies for her pocketbook, Mrs. St. John left.

"You can read your letter now," she said as Helen was closing the door.

Helen smiled. For someone as much in the dark as she was about her own daughter, Mrs. St. John was very perceptive. "Thank you," she said. "I will."

Dear Helen,

I hope you haven't given up on me! Sorry for the long wait on the letter, Honey, but we've had a [word blacked out] time of it these past few [word blacked out] and this is the first time I'm able to send a letter! Anyway, how are you, Honey? Still guarding the henhouse? Seriously, how are all the gals? I hope they are well. Gosh, I hope YOU are well!

We were pretty darn busy last month, but just before that, we had ourselves a real feast on some [word blacked out] specialties. They make some things with fish and tomatoes I never even heard of before. The fish I mean. My buddy Sly tells me how to pronounce them. I guess it's more natural to him, being Italian and all.

Is it getting pretty cold now? Gosh I miss you. I smelled a wood-burning fire the other night, and you guessed it, it brought back memories of our honeymoon. It's almost our silver, isn't it? Years go by. I miss you, Honey, all the time. I think what we're doing here is going to make us all strong, not just us men, but the whole United States. Some of the things that have gone wrong in the world are being righted. If you and the girls keep praying for us, and doing what you're doing, I know it will all come to a good end. I love you, Helen. Harry.

Helen closed the letter and held it close to her heart. She kissed it. She said a prayer of thanksgiving, sat peacefully for a few moments, then read the letter again.

Up 23rd, and down Arden Road, Joan had just brought in the mail herself. Annie jumped up when she saw the expression on Joan's face.

"Sylvester?"

"Maybe. . . " Joan teased. "Who's APO?"

"Gimme that!" Annie said, grabbing the letter. "I'll see you tomorrow."

"Oh! You think it'll be that good, huh? A nice long one with kisses and hugs?" Joan laughed.

"It better be after all this time!" She closed her door. Then, a second later, her head popped out. "Thanks, Joan."

> . . .Boy, Annie, you wouldn't believe the extremes in conditions. Not 3 weeks ago, Cap and I were having [word blacked out] and tomatoes, you know [word blacked out] style. Lots of it, too! If it weren't for the heavy activity, I might have gained a couple pounds. Then this week, over here, there's K rations, and that's it. We only see a bottle of beer or a draft mug on Saturdays. But I'll live. There's been quite a lot going on, though. I didn't tell you that [words blacked out] and that was only half the fun. I went out on a mission and got [word blacked out]. I'm doing okay, and Cap got me and him assigned at the same place. Isn't that great?
>
> Boy I miss you, Annie. I miss everything. I miss New Jersey. If you can believe it, I even miss school. Now that's saying something! A lot of the guys

*smoke and they say it keeps them from missing
everyone as much. I don't see how that's possible.
Cap says it's a bad habit, don't start. If you do, you
can't quit. I don't think much of smoking anyway.
How about you, babe?*

*I have to get to bed early. Tomorrow we're
[words blacked out], but as soon as I heard we could
send letters again, I got this pen and paper and
started this one to you. I can't wait for the day that
we see each other again! I'm saving a hundred
kisses, got em there in my rucksack.*

"Rise and shine!" called Harry, rapping on the
dormitory door. "Come on guys. Chow."

It was 4:30 am, November 15, 1943. For the tenth
day in a row, the linguists were set to listen to and
interpret the responses of prisoners who were being
interrogated by the Navy and Army Intelligence.
Sylvester, whose people, and hence their dialect, was
northern Italian, was one of five men who roomed in
a partially burned out apartment on the island of
Pantelleria.

Some of the fellows were there to provide
security, some were on recon for buried mines and
what was loosely called *cleanup.* But Sylvester and
Bobby Pitro were there to provide a running
interpretation as the prisoners responded. Before
any given day was up, both men would have
interpreted for at least 10 hours, often 12, with no
break. Since Italy's surrender, prisoners were happily
presenting themselves to be incarcerated. At first it

shocked Sylvester, but as time wore on, he'd learned that a prisoner in an Allied Camp ate better and was far safer than he was on the streets, or even at home. Starvation was rampant.   Most of the prisoners he listened to were not of a rank or intelligence level to be of much use to the strategic team, but each story was nevertheless interesting.   He learned how desolate the opposition's conditions were. While the soldiers garnered respect from the citizens, they were not well provided for, and toward the second surrender in 1943, some were not provided for at all. The stories were similar from soldier to soldier. "I found a lump of discarded pasta," he interpreted one day, "and I shared it with my three compadres. It was the first thing we had to eat in two days."

"How can this kind of stuff possibly help Intelligence?" Sylvester had wondered one night after work.

"You never know," Harry had said. "It may seem like nothing to you, but Intelligence can establish patterns of information that make it possible for them to predict what might be in store for us. Don't think your job isn't important."

And he had not. In fact, he became expert at the practice and was eventually called on to make a report for the team, making notes and gathering the similarities, pointing out the differences and making note of which soldiers in which regiments, under which leaders, had varying reports.

"You got the report ready?" Harry asked one day as Sylvester opened the door.

"Yep. Hey, it looks like the others are already out," Sylvester said, looking at three empty beds.

"Yeah, they are out for 12-hour duty next few days," Harry said. "It's just you and Bobby today."

"I'm ready," said Bobby.

Bobby was twenty-two and a junior at Vanderbilt University. He had a sweetheart to whom he had proposed in a letter, and gotten a big Yes in a letter back. He was hoping against hope to get leave at Christmas, and everyone was pulling for him. He was young looking for his age, but a handsome man, well-built and sure on his feet. If it hadn't been for his language ability, he would have made an excellent field soldier or even paratrooper.

"How's the leg, Bapini?"

"Good," Sylvester answered. "I bet you can't even tell anymore. Alls I got is a scar that's a little puffy. I walk all right, don't I?

"Hell yeah!" said Bobby.

"Come on," said Harry. "Somebody said they got some of that Italian coffee in. Come from Mussolini's private stash."

As they headed down the narrow hallway to the stairwell, Sylvester surveyed the group. "What a crew we make!" he said laughing. "You sure you want to be seen with us?"

"Yeah, have a little respect," Harry said.

"What are you doing today?" Sylvester asked. "Still making notes?"

"No, I gotta take that report you've done and add it to my stuff. There's another guy gonna take notes.

I'm supposed to, well, I've got an assignment, let's say."

Bobby and Sylvester looked at each other. *Assignment* was Harry's code word for top secret mission. Since the beginning of his service in the war, Harry's maintenance duties were of a peculiar nature. In fact, the only thing he maintained was top secret material.

His voyages between the VI Corps' Major General Truscott and receivership in General Clark's headquarters were flawless. He looked exactly like the maintenance man his title and credentials described him as. He spoke like a maintenance man. There was not a single clue about him that would render him likely intelligence. He was the perfect phantom, in maintenance clothing.

Harry's messages of the past had been carried only in his brain; he had no secret notes or code or cargo. It was simply a vocalized message, rapid and clear, under the guise of maintaining a telegraph or telephone set. Harry could work on the modern washing machine, all kitchen appliances, and most any car engine, in actual fact. But those skills were not being utilized at all.

On that special mission, Harry would carry actual documents. That mere fact ranked his mission extremely perilous. And to add to the challenge, while Harry had traveled through pockets of German territory in the past, his next journey would have him deliver these documents to General Clark's attaché in

Western Italy, the Gustav Line at the Garigliano
River, inside German held territory.

Bobby pulled out a chair for him. "Get you a
coffee?"

"Thank you, Lt. Pitro," Harry said, taking a seat.
"That's what I call respect."

Sylvester was already at the queue, signaling
"three" with his fingers in the air to the Italian fellow
behind the counter. The room was abuzz, and the
coffee did nothing to settle it.

"What's going on?" asked Sylvester as he came
back with the expressos. "Everyone seems pretty
energized for 4:45 in the morning! Don't tell me it's
the coffee."

"No. They'll tell you at muster," said Harry, "but
there's a lot going on. For one thing, looks like the
English, or most of them, will be moving out. They've
got something planned for later in the month, I hear."

"Up north?"

"I guess."

"You couldn't say if you knew, could you Cap?"
said Bobby.

"No." Harry took a sip. He leaned back to take in
the pleasure of the expresso. Just then, an explosion
took out an entire window, frame and all, and a
portion of the already degraded floor at the far end of
the room.

"What the hell!" Bobby shot up, eyes wide.

Harry and Sylvester got up just in time for a
British soldier to pop his head up at that window and
wave them back. "Stay back," he said, waving away

the smoke. "Mine went off. No casualties, but there may be more. Just exit out the other way, quickly please."

"Well, I wasn't really in the mood for a coffee anyway," said Sylvester as they headed out to work.

"Yeah, who needs coffee?" said Bobby. "We're men. United States Navy."

"Don't forget the Army," said Harry. "You all aint nothin' without the U.S. Army!"

A couple of Brits in line turned to add their remarks as Sylvester gave Harry a quick handshake. "Take care of yourself, buddy."

"I'll do my best."

Outside the building, Harry went west as Bobby and Sylvester went east.

Chapter Ten

"How about us both getting a letter the same day?" said Annie. "God was listening."

Helen mused. "I was thinking the same thing. Say, Annie, do you or anyone ever call Sylvester *Sly*?"

"What? Sly? No. Well, I don't. You gotta remember, I don't know his people yet. Maybe they do. What makes you ask?"

"Yeah, Helen, what's it to ya?" Bernice said, imitating Annie's accent.

"Watch it, Shortie," said Annie.

"Because Harry mentioned someone named Sly in his letter. I figure if they're both in Italy. . ."

"That's kind of a long shot, isn't it?" Joan's head appeared at the kitchen doorway.

"Yes, I'm sure it's someone else," said Helen. "I guess Italy's big enough for two Sylvesters."

"Oh," said Bernice. "So Sly is a nickname for Sylvester."

"Yeah," said Annie. "Don't you know anything?"

"Hey!"

Joan sat down. "Well I've never heard that."

"I heard of it, I read it in a book," said Helen. "The Captain of Bisori, or something like that."

"Speaking of 'Captain,'" said Annie. "Sylvester's always mentioning Cap or Captain. Could you pass me the cream, please?"

The four had gathered for a planning session. With the Thanksgiving Dance not far off, three of Helen's Sodality friends had become ill, leaving Helen to pick up the slack. Rather than go through the business of getting new people together, Helen just opted to ask the girls to help out. They were thrilled.

"I guess we'd better get started," said Helen. "I've got a notebook here with a page for each item we need to manage, the names of folks that we've contacted for it for past events, and their telephone numbers and addresses. Each of you will have her own page. Copy the information down, though, so we can keep everything together here."

"I call the refreshments," said Annie.

"Okay, good start," said Helen. "That's a very big responsibility, and you're familiar with what all the pitfalls can be. It's important to think ahead."

"Wow, Helen. You should be a teacher," said Bernice.

"Thanks Bernice. I was, you know, before I married Harry."

"No kidding!" said Joan. "I never knew that!"

"Well, you learn something new every day," said Annie. "What else you got there?"

"I'm handling the building and all of the things that go with that," Helen said, "just because I've done it before. But Joan, how about if you handle the entertainment, and Bernice, you handle the publicity? Does that suit you gals?"

They eagerly copied down the respective numbers and chatted excitedly about ideas and plans. "What about the bazaar?" asked Joan. "Is that still the week after?"

"Well, that's the 8th," said Helen. "Our dance is Friday, the 19th of November, so it's the middle of the week after next on the Wednesday. That's the best day for the housewives, being the middle of the week, you know. And with Advent starting, we don't want it on the weekend. Plus everyone will be coming for Mass on the 8th anyway, so we'll have lots of folks coming."

"In the meantime, has anyone gotten anywhere with these?" Annie pulled from her bag the start of her hostess dress.

"Believe it or not," began Bernice.

"You made a bed sheet by mistake," cut in Annie.

"I will ignore that," said Bernice. "I was going to say that believe it or not, I have actually cut out the pieces and they seem to match the pattern."

"That's great, Bernice!" Joan said. "I've just barely cut mine out myself. I didn't have the money for the material until night before last."

"That slowed us both down," said Annie. "But yours is so pretty, or going to be anyway. Helen, how about you?"

"You know, I was imagining what kind of a dress Harry would like to see me in," Helen said. "He was always partial to the prints—"

"*Was* always partial?" asked Bernice. "What do you mean? He's okay isn't he?"

"Oh yes, yes, I'm sorry," said Helen. "When I was figuring out what it would look like, I sort of--" she got a little flustered and grabbed for her hankie.

Joan and Annie exchanged glances. Bernice put a hand on her shoulder. "It's okay, Helen," she said.

"I guess it gets to me. No matter how old and crusty you are," she tried to laugh, "it still worries you, worries us gals back at home. But what I was trying to say was that I was just imagining maybe what Harry would want me to wear, want me to make." She looked kindly at Bernice. "I'm okay, Honey. Thanks." And she patted her hand.

Joan sighed. "This is such an incredibly hard time," she said, looking down at her hands.

"Yeah, wait until Dick gets overseas," said Annie, her voice cracking. "It'll be a lot harder then."

"Hey, what time is it?" asked Bernice.

"Well, *you're* the depths of compassion," said Annie.

"No, I just want to know if we have time to get to vespers. That's just what we need."

Annie and Joan looked at Helen, surprised. Helen did not return the look and just casually said, "I think that's a great idea. Can you all stay for dinner? We'll come back after and work on our dresses."

"We can," said Joan, "you, too, right, Bernice?"

"Yeah, sure," she said looking at Helen peculiarly.

"Well if you have to go," Helen said, "I understand."

"No," Bernice nodded, "I'd like to be here."

Annie looked at Joan with confusion but neither said anything.

"Well, great," said Helen, "let's grab our hats. It's almost four."

On the steps as the girls were leaving St. Benedict's, Margaret stood speaking to Dominic. As they neared the two of them, Bernice began to separate herself from the group. Margaret's boss then approached Margaret, engaging her in conversation. Dominic turned, recognizing the girls from their meeting at the dance.

"Hey girls," he said, nodding and smoothing back his hair. "How's it going?" When he spotted Bernice, though, he called out, "Hey there Bern! What a surprise to see you *here!*"

"Uh, you're the fellow from the bakery, aren't you?" asked Helen as Annie and Joan stared at Bernice who stood at the base of the steps and waved. "Calabria's, isn't it?" Helen continued.

"Uh well, yeah," Dominic answered, torn between trying to be polite and not wanting Bernice to get away. "We got the two stores, both in downtown. Hey Bernice!"

Bernice had made her way into the crowd, and Helen continued valiantly on. "Well it must be nice to have a family business, especially these days. Do you find it hard to get supplies?"

"No, we got, you know connections, well, you know, we are familiar with some of the uh. . .

suppliers," he said, giving up on Bernice, and turning to give Helen more respectful attention.

"Okay, well anyway, nice to see you," said Helen smiling and turning to the other girls. "Annie, Joan, are you two all right? Let's move along, we've got dinner!"

Bernice left a note on Helen's door that her mom and she were going to have dinner together. Helen did not seem very disappointed or even surprised, and when Annie broached the subject of Dominic, she seemed oblivious to there having been anything strange in it at all. Joan decided best to just drop it. These days, she thought, you never know what's happening.

But on the walk home, Annie could not resist. "So is it just me, or was there something weird in the way that guy Dominic was acting?"

"And Bernice!" said Joan.

"And what did he mean by 'what a surprise to see *you* here'?"

"He didn't say '*you* here,' he said 'you *here,*'" corrected Joan.

"Huh?"

"I mean he put the emphasis on the word *here*, not the word *you*," Joan said. "Do you understand what I mean?"

"Oh, okay, so it was more like what are you doing around here?"

"Yes, exactly."

They walked in silence for a few moments.

After a while, Annie threw up her hands. "Well I'm stumped."

"Yeah, I mean it's not like Bernice doesn't go to vespers a lot. Sometimes she goes even when we don't. In fact, today, it was her idea!" said Joan.

"No, no, that's not it," Annie said. "I, sorry, I didn't mean to be rude. I don't think he meant here, as in here at St. Benedict's."

"No?"

"No, I mean, I thought he meant something like here in town."

They walked a few more moments in silence.

"Well he's from Philly," said Joan. "Do you think he's seen her there, maybe with her boyfriend?"

"First of all, we don't know she's got a boyfriend," Annie said, "only that she's very secretive. What on earth. . . Do you think *he* is the boyfriend?"

"But he's Margaret's, isn't he?" said Joan. "Oh! Do you think he's two-timing? Do you think that could be why Bernice doesn't say anything? She knows she's with a two-timer?"

They were at their front door. Annie's eyes grew wide. "I'll bet you're right," she said. "Or else why would Bernice have run off like that?"

"That guy's pretty dumb, then," said Joan flatly.

Annie burst out laughing.

"What's so funny?"

"I don't know, you just don't say stuff like that very often," Annie said. "Kind of busted me up."

"You're wearing off on me, Annie."

Bernice was already at Helen's house when the four met the next day to work on their dresses.

"Thick as thieves, huh?" kidded Annie as she came in the door.

"I don't know about that," said Helen, "but we've got a surprise for you!"

"I love surprises!" Joan said, taking off her coat. "Is it sweet?"

"Yep!" said Bernice, "sweet and rich!" She took the kitchen towel off of a long metal tray and underneath lay an entire tray of freshly pressed chocolate fudge.

"Oh my gosh!" cried Joan. "That looks like heaven!"

"You guys can be thick as thieves any time you like," said Annie, venturing to take a piece.

"Uh uh uh!" said Bernice. "Wait 'til you're served. Most of this is going to the men, you know."

"Can't I just take a little crumb?"

"No."

Joan giggled. "I'll set the table."

"Thanks Joan," said Helen as she unfurled a fresh tablecloth, snapping it in the air before it gently fell into place onto the table. "I thought we would get out a fresh tablecloth in honor of Bernice's creation."

"Bernice's?" said Annie, making a face.

"Oh, okay," said Bernice. "Never mind then. None for you if you're going to be that way about it."

"No, no, no! Just joking!" said Annie.

With the blue and white china tea cups and saucers on Helen's silvery white linen table cloth, and the kettle ready to pour, everyone took a seat to sample Bernice St. John's and Helen Ashenbach's marvelous fudge. "Now don't expect too much," she said.

"Don't be silly, Bernice," Helen said. "We have already sampled it. It's fantastic!"

"No fair!" cried Annie.

"Cooks' privilege," said Helen, nodding at Bernice.

"Yes, indeed," said Bernice. "Here, one for each of you."

Joan sat back, anticipating it. "It's been so long since I've had anything this rich," she said. "I just want to savor the moment."

"Your mother makes a wonderful pan of fudge," said Helen.

"She sure does! But she and Daddy are giving it up, you know, until the War is won."

Bernice and Helen exchanged glances.

"Okay, what was that about?" demanded Annie.

"What?"

"That look—you two are in cahoots about something."

"Oh," Helen chuckled. "We were just talking about exactly that. About how the sacrificing that the nuns are doing, at well, all the nuns, really, has to be helping. There are so many battles being fought and many of them are being won by our boys. And sacrificing is one of the main causes, we have agreed."

Joan looked at her beautiful chunk of smooth, rich
chocolate fudge, a ridge of it piled high where the
knife had sliced it from the rest of the pan, and a few
crumbs still warm, tumbled around it. She looked up
at Helen, and then Bernice. She looked down at her
hands and shook her head. "Oh Helen, Bernice, I
really do want it, but you are right. Let's set this
aside, add it to the rest for the boys. I can't stand
there and fight alongside them, but at least I can
make small sacrifices."

"Are you nuts?" said Annie. She picked up her
piece, opened her mouth, looked at it and held her
pose, fudge in midair, mouth open, eyes glued to it,
and just as if her guardian angel had tapped her on
the shoulder, saying, "Oh Anne!" she set it back
down. Picked up the plate and handed it to Bernice.
"Okay, okay, get it outta here."

Everybody laughed. Bernice put the fudge back
with the rest in the tray, covered it up, and suddenly
the room was filled with the light and easy feeling
they hadn't known since before the War had started.
Helen poured the tea and they sat chatting and
laughing, and later pinning and stitching, putting
together their hostess dresses.

Chapter Eleven

The scent of the candlewax hung in the air like a blanket around Bernice, the flickering silence straight ahead as she knelt in the first pew. It was just a visit. She smiled. *Just* a visit. She'd heard Helen say, "I just went for a visit," or Joan, "just a visit, no Mass or anything," and even Annie, "no, we were just there for a visit."

In the deep silence, where it felt as if an angel of love wrapped its feathery wings around her, Bernice had grown to adore these "just visits," void of external conversation, and filled, utterly *filled*, with an ecstasy she could never describe. Minutes would pass, an hour, and she was always startled when the door opened or someone sat down next to her, bringing her back to the world as it was.

In the recent months, she'd found herself more and more drawn to these quiet and embracing moments with God. They were not an escape. They were not disruptive to her life. Rather, they were nourishment and life, rich, and life-sustaining. She sensed they sustained a life deeper than the one she had known so far in her nineteen years.

She breathed in and exhaled. Just then she heard sounds from way back in the choir loft, rattling of papers and the shuffling through pages of books and finally the soft chords of the organ as Bitsy familiarized herself with the hymns for the following Sunday's Mass. She had played the organ for St.

Benedict's for nearly 40 years, but still, every week, she would review the music to the hymns that she would play the following Sunday. Bernice had it right. She supposed Bitsy was just as much in love with the Church as she was, and just wanted to be inside its doors as often as she logically could. But unlike Bernice, Bitsy hadn't realized she didn't need a reason to come in.

Bernice turned her head and called up to Bitsy. "Is that a new one?" she asked, tongue in cheek.

"Oh hi, Bernice. I thought that was your head," said Bitsy.

"My head and the rest of me, too."

"No, it's not new. We've done it before. Why don't you come up?"

"I'm on my way!" Bernice said. Bitsy did not have to ask twice.

Father Bertrand could hear music coming from the church and smiled. That was one thing that always brought him joy. He would always be grateful for Bitsy. She had been through many years with St. Benedict's and had never wavered in her excellent musicianship. She had a little bit of an edge as the choir director, and there had been quite a few tears shed from the harsh things she'd said, but everyone had faults, he reasoned. And things always seemed to work out in the end, one or the other giving in, usually the other.

He rose from his knees. To one side of his living and dining room area, he had set up a prayer table, adorned with a beautiful gold and white linen covering given to him by Helen's Sodality Club, upon which rested a statue of the Holy Family. He paused to look into the face of St. Joseph, one wistful moment on behalf of his dear, lost friend.

Nothing had been communicated from or even about Father Kuchesky in a very long time. Father Bertrand knew that it was unreasonable to expect that his friend was all right, considering the Nazi atrocities he had read about, if those reports were accurate. Alphonse would never simply stop corresponding with his friends in the United States, especially in view of how they would worry about him, if he were able. The Polish newspapers reported the existence of mass graves filled with people who were simply lined up and shot, then pushed into the dirt as if a herd of diseased cattle. It so sickened Father Bertrand that he could never meditate on it, and speak of it only in a very detached way.

The November day had turned brisk, and Father pulled his coat close as he stepped into the windy corridor between the rectory and church. The music grew louder as he approached the church doors. Who was singing? Wasn't it Bernice, the one that he'd heard last week? She had quite a talent.

The music came to an abrupt halt as he opened the side door and stepped inside. "Oh no, please don't stop on my account," he said. "It's beautiful! Bernice, is that you?"

"Good afternoon, Father, yes, it is. Thank you!"

"I hope we hear from you at Midnight Mass," he said smiling at Bitsy. Then he headed to the sacristy to prepare for the vespers.

"You heard him," said Bitsy. "It's not just me. Oh, won't you sing it for Midnight Mass? It's just beautiful, Bernice."

"I'll be in the choir," said Bernice. "You know that. But this is my first year. I don't want to be some young upstart."

Bitsy laughed. "I don't know about that," she said. "But one thing for sure, nobody can argue that you aren't the one for the song."

Bernice looked up sharply. "What do you mean? Is there someone else who is supposed to sing it?"

"Well, Carol's always done it," Bitsy said, shaking her head. "But honestly, it might be nice to have a pretty new voice this year. I think she's ready for a rest."

Suddenly the prospect of singing the song for Christmas grew nebulous. "*She's* ready for a rest, or . . ." her voice trailed off. Bernice did not quite know how to finish the question.

"Oh no, she, yes. I just meant she's probably tired of doing it," said Bitsy, who suddenly needed to rifle through music on the far side of the organ.

Bernice was not convinced, but they rehearsed the song once more before the rest of the choir members started to arrive.

Dick grabbed a booth by the door and ordered a cup of coffee. The Tastee Diner was a great spot. He

had loved it all his life, the smell of the eggs on the
grill, the bacon, and those wonderful fried potatoes.
Why oh why couldn't his mother figure out how to
make them like that?

"You got somebody else coming?" the waitress
said as she slapped the cup down on the table. A little
coffee jostled onto the saucer.

"Oh, yes. Yes, one more party, thank you," said
Dick. "Have you got any—"

"Cream's on its way," she said flatly.

Just then a fellow from inside the counter area
passed a glass pitcher with a metal top across to her.
She turned and grabbed it, and set it with great
decisiveness onto Dick's table. "There's your cream."

"Yes indeed," Dick said. "Thank you. I expect
we'll be ready to order shortly after the rest of my
party arrives."

The waitress moved on to the next table without a
word.

Dick smiled and shook his head. If there was
anything he could count on, it was that the wait staff
at the Tastee Diner would forever exhibit an
invariable degree of charm.

Bob popped in the door. "Hey, sorry I'm late,
buddy," he said. "Women." He laughed.

"Women? I thought you were engaged," said Dick
moving his coffee to the side.

"I am! That's the woman! You have to write them,
you know."

"Oh. Well. . ."

"You write to that cute little number Joanie, don't you?"

"Well, I have. . . I don't as a rule. . ."

"You better watch out, bud," Bob said.

"Watch out? Watch out for what?"

Bob laughed. "Don't you get it? You can't let a honey like that one swing in the wind. You don't seal the deal, or at least keep her reading your letters, you might as well kiss her goodbye."

"Hm," said Dick, thinking it over.

"What's good?" Bob asked.

"I'm getting it all," Dick said, "bacon, eggs, potatoes and toast."

"And coffee."

"And coffee."

"Sounds good," said Bob. "How are their eggs— are they the real thing?"

"Yeah, Boy."

"Count me in."

The same afternoon, Joan stood at the stove, waiting for the tea water to heat. "Did you get the fudge packaged and out to the boys?" she asked Helen.

"We sure did!" Helen said. "Oh I hope it gets to them in good shape. That batch was for the boys in Norfolk," she said. "Navy recruits."

"How do you choose who to send it to?"

"We don't choose, they just tell us after we hand it over. It depends on where there's a need. The recruits who will be away over Christmas, trainees, they'll be away for their first year, most of them, and missing their families. I guess the Navy figures every little bit helps."

"If it were me, it would help!" said Annie, dropping her grocery bags onto the table. "Guess what we brought?"

"Sugar, oh say 'sugar!'" said Helen. "Please!"

"Sugar!" said Annie, laughing.

"What wonderful news! I wasn't sure how we were going to do this. We only had 4 cups between us."

"Well, if we make our cakes for Christmas and freeze them," said Annie, "then we can use this," and she pulled out a two-pound sack, "for the dance. But we won't have any cookies this year. I'm told this is the end of the line."

"As long as there's cake," said Joan.

"Yes, cake will be plenty," said Helen. "What do we care about cookies? We're watching our figures anyway. Hey, where's Bernice?"

"Oh, get this," said Annie, "she is parking the car!"

Joan gasped. "But she doesn't know how to drive!" she said.

"She's decided she's going to learn," said Annie. "It's fine with me. She's a natural. She's just getting her stuff out. Everything's okay."

"It's *your* car," said Helen, laughing.

"Hey, I heard that!" called Bernice opening the door.

As Joan poured the tea, the girls sorted out the various projects they'd be doing that day, some for Christmas, some for the dance.

"What do you hear from Dick, Joan?" asked Helen.

Annie and Joan exchanged glances. "Well," said Annie, "she got a nice letter yesterday."

"You did?" said Helen smiling. "Come on, what did he say!"

"It was actually really nice," said Joan. "I was surprised. I mean he's written before, but he hasn't been so, you know, romantic."

"Oooh, romantic!" said Bernice.

"Oh hush," said Joan. "It was sweet, I don't know if romantic is the word, though. He said how he really enjoyed the time we'd spent together, which he had said before. And he said he would be coming to the dance, which is great. I was so relieved."

"Yeah, that's the main thing," said Annie. "I get the feeling Dick is more in person, not so much the letter writer."

"It's all so new to these fellows," said Helen. "They probably never expected to have to write letters wooing a woman. They have to get up to speed."

"Just like the military," said Annie.

Helen nodded. "Yes, I guess they were caught off-guard there, too."

"So it's good," said Bernice. "He'll be coming, and you can rest easy that you'll see him. That's the main thing, right?"

Joan smiled at her. "You're right, Bernice."

"Speaking of letters," said Annie, looking at Helen. "This waiting game is getting old, isn't it? You haven't heard from Harry again, have you? Since that time, we both got a letter?"

Helen shook her head and looked at her lap. "No, I haven't," she said quietly. "But we've been through it before, you know, Annie."

"Yeah, well with Sylvester's good looks, and of course his ability to speak the language. . . "

"Oh my gosh!" cried Bernice. "Are you seriously concerned that he is two-timing you?"

"Well it wouldn't be the first time a man stepped out," said Annie.

"Annie, no!" said Joan. "He's engaged to you! He would never do such a thing!"

"Well what if he met some sexy Italian broad," said Annie, "and she, you know, vamps him or somethin'."

Helen and Bernice looked at each other and burst out laughing.

"You have *got* to be joking," said Bernice.

"Oh Honey, I just don't see it either," said Helen. "Not Sylvester. He loves you."

Annie looked a little challenged, but said nothing.

"You can't put any faith in that fear," said Joan, who was not laughing. "Sylvester just isn't the type." She gave Annie a hug. She sensed a vulnerability in her friend and it broke her heart. The tough, devil-may-care Annie had an Achilles Heel. Wasn't that how love was supposed to be? It changed you?

Softened you but toughened you up at the same
time?

Annie smiled at her, her eyes glistening slightly as
she dabbed at them. "Thanks," she said. "Thank you,
you two also. It's. . . rough."

"Well I would agree with that," Helen said. "I
don't mind telling you I'm worried. Italy is not the
easiest place to be right now." She reached her hands
out on each side of her, and instinctively the girls
formed a circle. They began to pray the Hail Mary.

Sylvester and Bobby stood at attention, listening
as their Commander spoke. "Captain Ashenbach has
been pulled for a special assignment, men, and we're
seeking a pair of volunteers to follow up in the
southeastern part of the country to help with
debriefing. As you know—"

Two hands shot up.

"You may want to hear this out," he said. "I
haven't given the description yet."

"No, Sir!"

"All right then, Bapini and Pitro, good men. I'll
have orders for you shortly. I hope you're seaworthy,
Pitro."

"Yes, Sir!"

The rest of the young men were clearly relieved.
For most, the unknown was a scary thing to
contemplate.

As the Commander left, Bobby and Sylvester
shook hands. "Well that'll get us out of here!"

Sylvester said. "With Cap gone, it's getting awful boring. I'm ready for a little more excitement."

"I'm with you," said Bobby.

They returned to quarters to pack up their gear with dreams of grandeur swirling in their heads.

"This came for you," said one of the guys, as Sylvester entered the barracks.

"Thanks, man." A letter from Annie. I better read this now, he thought. It's hard to know when I'll have another chance. He sat on the edge of his bunk and as he opened it, out fell two rectangular pieces of cloth connected by lengths of brown cording. He smiled and read on.

> " . . . *I know you're in God's hands out there, wherever you are, doing what you do, but this is a blessed scapular, of the Blessed Mother. I wear mine always. It reminds me of who I am, keeps my feet on the ground (as much as is possible!). I think it's very important. If you agree, this one is for you to wear."*

Sylvester smiled, felt the smooth brown cord of his own scapular, already on, kissed his new one and put it into his pocket.

Bernice listened to the organ play through the introduction. The sopranos and altos were up at the rail, the tenors and baritones slightly behind, and she, Bernice, right in the middle of it all. As the piece began, the sopranos sang the beautiful melody, flanked by the gentle alto line, and echoed by the tenors and baritones in unison with each other for the start. Then as it took off, all four parts blossomed into a gorgeous counterpart. It was an awe inspiring experience. Every time.

Bernice could never take it for granted. She felt as if by the beauty of their voices, and the glory of the song itself, she was being lifted up on a cloud. Then came the eight measures that preceded her part, and at last her solo. Just her voice and the organ. The organ chords came softer in this section, and her voice, pure, and clear as a bell did not fail her.

When her solo was over, the choir recommenced and she stepped into the soprano section to sing with them for the rest of the piece.

"Beautiful, Bernice," said one of the altos. "Really good singing!"

"Thank you," Bernice whispered. "It's the song. It's beautiful."

As she turned back, she caught the tail end of a mocking gesture by Carol to the soprano next to her. Carol did not realize she'd been caught, and Bernice did not let on. Carol and the girl next to her giggled amongst themselves, secure in the belief that it was their own private joke.

"What a day," said Annie as she clomped into the kitchen. "It sure smells good in here, though. Whatcha got cooking?"

"Do you remember that mush Helen gave me last week?" Joan asked. "It looked so good, I decided to try it the way this book says, and make it up with some scrapple on the side."

"That sounds good. I've never had it before, but it sounds good."

"Yeah. I think you'll like it. Mom gave me a little of her applesauce, too."

"Mmm. How are your parents?"

"Good. Yours?"

"Good, too. My uncle may be coming home on leave."

"Wow that's nice. I hope he can."

Joan brought the dinner to the table as Annie put her coat and pocketbook away.

After grace, Annie interjected, "Queen of Peace."

"Pray for us."

They ate amiably for a while, and then Joan said, "Annie, I have a feeling you're not really worried that Sylvester is going to find himself an Italian floozy."

"Oh yeah?" Annie said.

"Yeah," said Joan. "First of all, nobody thinks he's that type, and second, he's in a combat zone. I don't think floozies stand around and flaunt themselves in combat zones."

Annie burst out laughing.

"I'm trying to be serious," said Joan. "And third, you shouldn't think of Sylvester that way. He doesn't deserve it."

Annie put down her fork and took a deep breath. "I know it," she said. "You're right, Joan."

"So you never believed it anyway, huh?"

"No."

They started eating again.

"I mean, it's more like you'd find a Chinese elephant in Peru," Joan went on.

Annie smiled. "I know you're trying to make me say it," she said. "But I feel that if I do, it will be real, and so far, it's all in my mind."

Joan sighed. "You're worried he's in danger."

"More than that. I'm worried he's hurt, or is going to get hurt. He never explained why he hadn't been able to write before. Then all of the sudden, he wrote and it was glorious! Then, and just like Harry, I might add, nothing! Oh Joanie, it's killing me!" Annie covered her face with her hands and turned away.

Joan went to her side of the table to comfort her. "You are so good, Annie. No matter what happens, you will be happy again."

Annie snuffed and wiped her eyes. "You're the good one, Joan," she said.

Joan leaned back and smiled and said, "No, you're gooder."

A little way away, Helen sat at her dining room table, surrounded by shells and glue, boxes of backings and cotton balls. Her radio played and dinner baked warmly in the oven. Just then a song came on the radio, a familiar and beloved song, I Walk Alone. Helen instantly became transported to a calmer time just before Harry had signed up. She'd put on her red and black print, and they had held hands, walking to the corner store. Thinking back, she realized he must have known he was going to sign up. Why else all the romance?

"How about a dance?" he'd said as they came home. And just as he'd turned on the radio, that song came on. "I Walk Alone," he had sung along, trying to be funny. Helen had felt like a newlywed.

"You're crazy!" she'd laughed.

They'd danced for a while, and later that night, as the stars shone in the clear sky, he and Helen had tried to count them.

She stepped away from the table and shut off the kitchen light so she could move the curtain in the window without light coming through. There they were. All 89 stars. "Oh dear God," she prayed, "please keep him safe!"

Chapter Twelve

November 20th arrived at last, bringing with it the crunch of October's leaves mixed with the chill of winter. The elderly oaks around Helen's home swayed and groaned in the night, their endurance tested by the wind that whipped between the houses and through the leaf scattered streets. The Thanksgiving Day Dance, for which Helen fully intended to give thanks, had also arrived, bringing with it the hopes and dreams of her younger friend, Joan. Would Dick follow through, she wondered. He seemed like a very nice fellow, and steady, too. But he wasn't the impulsive type, and he had shown great reserve throughout his and Joan's courtship so far.

Helen retrieved four large trays from the deep freeze. That freezer was the one luxury Harry had been able to afford and what a treasure it had turned out to be. Between hers and the one in St. Benedict's, they'd successfully made enough cookies and snacks to provide for the whole dance. She smiled. In her day, the dances had been fewer, and the only refreshment she could remember was tea or punch. These dances were actually more like surrogate meals for so many of the kids attending. The men in training, the gals living at home with just a little less than enough to eat, and the working men and women both who even if they'd had enough, didn't have enough ration tickets for much of anything in between meals.

Annie's bakery connection had been a godsend, thought Helen, setting the trays on the kitchen table. Where would they ever have gotten sugar enough for all of this! She thought of the boys in Virginia who would be getting Bernice's wonderful home-cooked fudge soon enough. That was just as much a gift to the four girls as it was to the men. Then there was Joan, who was nervous enough about her own possible future with Dick, but yet her heart went out to her friend Annie, suffering the torment of wondering, not knowing, fearing where and how Sylvester was. Helen knew the fear. She'd felt it herself as a young woman. And she felt it now. But she was somehow protected this time, safe in the warmest friendship and love she'd ever known throughout her life. No matter what happened, she would be all right. She would be supported by the strength surrounding her. She knew that.

It was a day of thanksgiving, even if the actual holiday had not yet arrived. The dance would be a wonderful way to celebrate the holiday.

Joan stood in her slip, her hair still pinned up, penciling in her eyebrows. "I feel like I look like one of those cartoons," she said, frustrated and setting down the pencil. "I am just messing everything up!"

Annie leaned over to look at her reflection, then she turned and looked at her actual eyebrows. "I don't think they look bad. Just smudge this bit off," she said, wetting her thumb and wiping away a misshapen corner of Joan's left eyebrow. "There."

"I wish I were ambidextrous," said Joan. "That's why I do that one poorly all the time. I can't work on that side. Thanks."

"Don't let your nerves get the best of you, Joanie," said Annie. She was dressed in the pretty blue dress she'd lent Joan before. The stain from Miss Redhead's drink had come out just fine, and with her height, it looked like a completely different dress on Annie. Her face had rarely needed much makeup. Her eyebrows were already "made up," having grown in a sleek line just exactly at the brow bone with a slight arch. Her cheekbones were set apart enough so that they created a natural indent just under them. Joan always said she didn't even need lipstick, but Annie wore it for special occasions, and face powder, too.

Bernice stepped in the front door. "Is that what you're wearing?" she said to Joan.

Joan put down her pencil, sighed, and went into her room.

"What'd I say?" Bernice asked, setting her pocketbook down and unbuttoning her coat.

"She's just nervous. You didn't say anything," said Annie. "Come on in. Let's get these pigs boxed up."

"Oh golly, Annie! At least call them pigs in a blanket! Pigs. Ew." Bernice shuddered.

Annie laughed. "Okay, pigs within bedding," she said.

"No, livestock. Livestock within bedding," Bernice amended.

"Livestock within crinoline," laughed Annie. "Stuffed within."

They continued to outdo each other until Joan walked in in her robe and asked, "What in the world are you talking about?"

Annie lifted a pig-in-a-blanket, and offered it to her, saying, "Could you possibly enjoy livestock under cover of a worsted wool comforter?"

"What?"

The phone rang and Bernice answered it. "Oh hiya Helen! . . . Yes, well mostly, but I think Joan's going in her slip. . . yeah, okay. Bye bye."

"Very funny," said Joan, sharply.

"Well, that's what you had on the last time I saw you."

"I'm not going in my slip!" she said. Then with a sly smile, "I'm going in my robe."

The night air was cold but clear, and the stars were in their glory. Annie scurried across the parking lot, wondering what kind of skies were over Sylvester and if they could see any of the same stars. Someone opened the door and she could hear the orchestra tuning up. What a sweet sound that was, music. Especially these days, music was such a gift. How could anyone possibly dwell on the unpleasant when instruments played in harmony and the notes flashed and fluttered? She gave one last longing look at the starlit sky and entered the church hall, the door closing behind her.

"Thanks a lot," came a voice behind her.

"Oh Margaret! I didn't see you!"

"That's okay, I saw you daydreaming at the sky. I figured you'd slam the door on me."

"But I didn't, I—"

"Yes, you did, but that's okay. I brought the flyers for the Bazaar."

"That's great!"

"I know. I'll put some on a chair here and then some up front."

"Where's your Dominic?"

"He belongs to the baker," she said passively. "I don't know if he's coming. I can just hang around with you guys."

Joan and Bernice arrived. "We carried everything in," she said, "but we need some chairs from downstairs."

"Hello Joan," said Margaret.

"Oh hi," said Joan. "I didn't see you there. Sorry!"

"Hi Margaret," said Bernice.

"No, I didn't bring my Philly friend, in case you wanted to know," Margaret said to Joan, a little sharply.

"Oh, well I—"

Margaret stomped off. Joan and Annie looked at each other, then at Bernice. Bernice shrugged. "Let's go get the chairs," she said.

By 9:00, the dance was in full swing. The blackout windows were covered with Helen's decorations, which were quite a hit. She had created large crepe paper turkeys with larger crepe paper farmers running after them. But a bigger hit were the chicken legs, each of which was tied with a bow at the narrow end and had been fried in Annie's special blend of herbs.

"What's in this?" one young recruit asked.

"Secret spices," said Annie.

"Will you dance with me? Maybe I'll get it out of you on the dance floor."

Annie pointed to her left ring finger. "Engaged," she said.

"That's okay," he said. "I'm trustworthy."

Annie laughed and took his hand.

Joan smiled as they left for the dance floor. She was happy to see Annie dancing. Surely Sylvester wouldn't mind just a dance or two. After all, he had his floozy. She made herself giggle.

"Did you tell yourself a joke?" asked Margaret, who seemed to materialize out of nowhere.

"Oh hi, no I was just remembering something funny."

"You know boys do find me attractive," Margaret said.

"Well of course they do," said Joan. "You *are* attractive, so they would."

"Nah, don't patronize me," said Margaret, and slunk back into the shadows.

Joan turned toward her but she had completely disappeared. This is definitely a different kind of dance, she thought. Annie was dancing with the young fellow, her pretty, black hair and shiny, blue dress flashing in the low light. The music was very nice, and the orchestra had tossed in some Christmas classics for atmosphere. But where, she wondered, were Dick and his party? Where was Laureen for that matter? Had something happened? An accident maybe? But before she could get herself too worked up, Bernice stepped beside her.

"Hey there. What are you doing over here?"

"Just watching Annie. Isn't she pretty?"

"Yes. She really is. I have a feeling she doesn't actually know she's pretty, too, which makes her all the more so."

Joan smiled. "You're right Bernice. What a nice thing to say."

"Oh, every once in a while, I exercise a little charity," she said smiling. "We're back there." She pointed to Helen at the refreshment table. "Why don't you spend some time with the home team?"

Joan laughed and followed her back. "You think Dick will ever show?" she asked Helen.

"If he said he's coming, he means to come."

"That's right," said Bernice. "It could be extra slow going you know. All the soldiers on the road and all. Besides they probably had to wait until the rest of the guys were ready."

"Yes," said Helen. "That and the weekend. People like to be out on the weekend."

Joan smiled. She could tell her friends were trying to make her feel better. "You're probably right," she said, knowing people might like to be out, but gas rations being as they were, it wasn't always an option.

Just then she spotted Laureen. "Just a second, girls," she said. The music had stopped and she called to Laureen. Laureen smiled and approached her. She wore a pink tea length off-the-shoulder dress with a beautiful white corsage.

"Hi Joan!" she called reaching out to grasp her friend's hands. "I bet you thought they weren't coming!"

Joan laughed. "I was getting worried." She looked past Laureen but didn't see Bob or Dick.

"It's my fault," Laureen continued. "We had to drop off my mom in Linwood, and then we had to find a ration ticket between the 3 of us because we were almost out of gas. Luckily Dick had one, and finally we made it." She paused and looked around. "It's beautiful! Did you do all this?"

"Oh, golly no," said Joan. "Helen and her Sodality Club. We just made some of the refreshments. Uh, I wonder. . . "

"They're parking the car," said Laureen. "Don't worry. I didn't leave them home!"

Joan giggled and motioned for Laureen to get something to eat. "You remember Laureen," she said to Helen.

"I sure do. Hi, Honey," said Helen. "Help yourself.

As they talked, Joan glanced up at the crowd of girls lining the row of windows in the hall. Wall flowers. Her heart twinged for them. She flashed back for a second to the night of the Atlantic City affair when she'd been among the hopeful many, anticipating, dreaming of finding someone special. And then she had. He made her heart sing, and her head light with anticipation. He was every quality she wanted in a man. The only problem was he wasn't quite hers. . . yet.

Laureen tapped her on the shoulder, and she shook off her reverie. "Don't look now," she said, "but we've got company!"

There they were; tall, looking strong, in their service uniforms, hats in hand and smiles on their faces. Laureen and Joan stood like well-dressed statues, taking it all in. Joan felt like giggling. She stopped herself, but just barely. Laureen jabbed her in the elbow, giggling outright.

Margaret, catching sight of the men approaching, sidled up to Helen. "Do you think Joan knows Dick is here?"

"She might," Helen said.

"I bet she thinks he'll propose," Margaret said loudly.

Annie quickly pulled Margaret aside so whatever else she came up with would not be universally heard. "Isn't it a nice party?" she said. "Let's look at the orchestra's instruments while they're taking a break—from a distance of course."

"Oh yes," said Margaret obliviously. "I enjoy examining the various components of a musical ensemble."

Helen sighed and looked to see if Joan had heard. She needn't have worried. Joan could have been standing next to a marching band passing through a tornado and still been unaffected. She was transfixed, her eyes glued to the tall, dark serviceman approaching in calm, deliberate strides. He wore the United States Army uniform better than anyone she'd ever seen. And his smile was warm and easy. Her natural inhibition made her want to look away, but something inside denied her, and their eyes were locked.

Bob reached Laureen a few steps before and broke the spell. "Hello, Joan, how are you?" he said, offering his hand.

Joan shook it, smiling at him, mute. Laureen giggled. Just as Bob was about to open his mouth again, Dick arrived and embraced Joan.

"Oh, it's so good to see you!" he said. "You look truly stunning."

Joan felt tears at the corners of her eyes. "Hello, Dick," she said, unable to come up with anything else but a smile.

"Sorry we were delayed," he said. "I see Laureen's found you, and maybe she explained, but we had a few stops to make once we got into town."

"Oh yes, she explained," Joan said nodding, still smiling.

"Did we miss much?"

"I don't know about you, Dick," Bob said, "but I'm hungry! Let's eat!"

After the boys, between them, had downed six chicken legs, seven homemade rolls, four thick slices of ham, four cups of scalloped potatoes, a quart of macaroni and cheese, and half a celery stick, Bob suggested they find a place to sit. Bernice had arrived with a large tray of the girls' homemade cookies, thawed and glistening in the lights.

"Oh, look at that!" said Dick. "Great stuff!"

"Thank you," said Margaret. "But I'm already taken for the next dance."

Bernice fought a hard battle with a giggle. Helen stomped on her foot.

"Uh, oh yes," said Dick. "Well, uh, pardon me. . . "

"Here's a spot," said Joan, who had missed the whole thing. "That group just left and there's space for all of us." She looked at Bernice. "What's so funny?"

"I think Bernice is nervous in front of men," Margaret said.

"Come on," Annie said pushing Joan ahead of her, making a face at Bernice over her shoulder. "Let's grab it before somebody else takes it."

Joan and Dick sat side by side, Laureen and Bob beside Dick, and Annie, Bernice, Helen, and Margaret beside Joan.

"This is cozy," said Annie. "And it sure is good to get off my feet!"

"Oh, that is for sure!" agreed Helen. "You don't know how tired you are until you sit down."

When the orchestra returned, Dick immediately asked Joan to dance. Bob and Laureen followed.

"So where's your young man tonight?" Helen asked Margaret.

"I don't know," Margaret answered, glaring at Bernice.

"Maybe he's stuck in traffic," Annie said, "like what happened to Bob and them."

"I don't believe traffic is a consideration at 9:00 at night," Margaret said. "But thank you for the suggestion, Annie. Do you have any, Bernice?"

"Traffic?" Bernice said.

"*Suggestions!*" Margaret corrected crossly.

"Margaret, honey, you're shouting," said Helen. "I'm sure Bernice can hear you."

A short, handsome Airman interrupted to ask Annie to dance, and just as they were heading for the floor, another asked Bernice.

"Sorry I gotta cut this short," Bernice said over her shoulder on the way to the dance floor. "I'll try to think of something while we're dancing."

"I would appreciate it," called Margaret.

Helen shook her head. "Well, I'd better get back to work. There's lots to do."

The tempo of the music had gently tumbled to a slow rhumba, and although neither Joan nor Dick knew the dance, they stayed on the dance floor. To Joan, it seemed as if they'd been there all night in a dream.

"Do you think we're fooling anybody?" Dick said.

"Hmm?"

"Are we making this look authentic?" he asked, swaying back and forth.

Joan laughed. "I don't know, but I don't care. I think we're doing just fine."

Dick could smell the perfume Joan wore and unlike other women's, it did not make him sneeze. Nor did it have the ill effect of the perfume worn by that woman he'd been set up with a couple of years ago. He remembered how sick to his stomach he'd gotten and shivered involuntarily.

Joan pulled back. "Are you all right? It is a little chilly in here."

"No, no," he said. "I was just remembering something."

"Couldn't have been that pleasant, I guess, if it makes you shudder."

"Yeah, I was remembering this gal's perfume—"

"What?"

"Oh, not like that, it actually made me sick. I was comparing it to yours—"

"Does mine make you sick? Oh, gee whiz!" said Joan, flustered.

"No, I meant yours is so nice by comparison."

Joan looked unconvinced.

"I really mean that. It was so heavy and overwhelming. I could hardly breathe. Yours is light, and it brings to mind some kind of spring blossoms. It's airy and at the same time has a floral scent."

Joan smiled and they went back to dancing.

At the end of the rhumba, they returned to the table where the boys decided to go fill their plates with goodies.

"He likes my perfume," said Joan.

"Oh," said Helen. "That's nice!"

"I read somewhere, "Annie said, "that when you think about remembering something or someone, the strongest trigger is the olefactory."

Bernice burst out laughing. "The what? The old factory? What are you talking about, Annie?"

"Not old factory," Helen chucked, "*olefactory*. I means the sense of smell."

"Oh. No kidding? I never heard of that."

"See, us downtown gals got something on the ball," Annie said.

"Yeah, probably cheese," said Bernice. "Where's he off to?"

"I don't know," Joan said, dabbing her nose looking into her compact. "He said he has to talk to Bob."

"Laureen's coming. She'll know," said Helen.

Joan thought about how she had become so dependent on Laureen, while not really knowing her any better than she had in grade school. She thought of how Laureen had not only sought her out back at the St. Nicholas Dance, but encouraged her, and then later, reinforced Dick's interest in her. She was like an angel. A romance angel, Joan thought, smiling to herself.

"What are you so deep in thought about?" asked Annie, handing her a cup of punch.

"More like who than what."

"Ooooh!" Annie said smiling.

"No, nothing like that. I was just thinking how great Laureen's been to me—and for no reason at all."

Annie smiled. "There's a reason," she said. "Laureen's a good person. And she knows without a doubt in her mind that you would be there for her if she needed you."

"I would be," Joan said looking at the floor.

"Did you lose an earring?" said Margaret.

Annie just shook her head smiling at Joan. "No."

When Laureen arrived, she explained that the boys were having a confab about who was driving and when they would leave to go back to Washington, D.C.

"Aren't they staying overnight?" Joan said.

"Not this time. There apparently are new restrictions on the amount of time they can be away. All I can think is that they're getting closer to their time and—"

"Oh, that makes my heart sink," said Joan clasping Laureen's hands.

"Mine, too. But I'm not allowed to react around Bob. It upsets him, but I think that's because *he* doesn't want *me* to get upset."

"I hope they can stay for another set," said Joan. "The orchestra is wonderful and Dick is such a good dancer."

As it turned out, Bob had wanted to leave and Dick had wanted to stay, so they compromised and decided to leave midway through the set.

"I have to go along with him," Dick explained. "He's the man with the wheels."

"Do you have a car, Dick?"

"No, I sold the one I had. I borrow Daddy's '39 Hudson when I'm in town. But since we're shipping out soon, there's no reason to get a car now."

"Oh, look, they're getting ready to start up again."

"That reminds me, I told Bob maybe we might have a dance with Mrs. Ashenbach," Dick said. "She is a real peach to do all this—oh and you and the gals, too! I didn't mean—"

"No, not at all!" laughed Joan, her eyes filled with admiration. "By all means, go and ask her if Bob doesn't beat you to it!"

Helen was a good dancer and Joan enjoyed watching the two of them waltz around the generous floor space. Just as the dance ended, Bob cut in, and Helen was off again on another dance. Dick reached out his hand for Joan, and she felt butterflies flapping their wings. It was that song again, I Don't Want to Set the World on Fire. This is it, she thought. He's been so attentive all night, and sharing every detail of his life. He's so suave, so romantic, and such a gentleman. He seems a little nervous. Oh, how will he ask me? Straight out, or make a little speech, and go on one knee. I wonder if he's got a ring box in his pocket, like Bob had for Laureen. Or if he'll wait and we'll go and pick it out together.

She smiled and reached out her hand and they danced as if floating in the clouds. She rested her head on his shoulder and he held her close. They barely noticed the one song leading into another. When Bob finally tapped Dick on the shoulder, Dick responded with, "No cutting in, fellow."

Bob laughed, but said, "We better get going. It's supposed to pour down rain in another few hours. I'd like to miss as much of that as we can."

This is it, thought Joan. Dick looked longingly into her eyes, waved to her friends at the table, and said, "I will remember this night forever." And he was off!

The two men headed casually for the door as if they were leaving to go buy a bottle of milk.

The next song started, but Joan just stood there in the middle of the floor, breathless, not sure if she were going to cry, and really hoping she wasn't. She knew people used different terminology in different parts of the country, but she was pretty darn sure that Dick's last words had not been a proposal in any region of the US. She turned as Annie put an arm around her and walked her to the side of the room.

Annie shrugged, and looked in the direction that Dick and Bob had gone. Suddenly her mouth dropped open in astonishment. Joan turned to look, and then wished she hadn't.

There at the exit, lying in wait like a crimson black widow, stood the odious redhead, her skinny body clad in a dreamy lime chiffon formal, with white flowers running through her hair. Her gloved white hand reached out for Dick as he passed.

He paused. Then he stopped. He began to talk to her. He was smiling and talking to her. Even *Bob* was talking to her! Joan looked to Laureen, but she had gone to the kitchen with Helen. Annie and Bernice stood stock still, just as shocked as she.

"Maybe she wants to know if he likes throw-up, like the color of her dress," said Annie.

"How in the world does she time things so perfectly?" asked Bernice.

"Well how long is he going to talk to her?" wailed Joan. "Oh come *on!*"

"Joanie, Joanie, it's going to be okay. It doesn't mean a thing," said Annie. "Look, he's leaving now."

"And he's waving to *her!*"

It was true. As they walked out the door, Dick waved to the redhead, who stood wiggling the fingers on her left hand up near her cheekbone, covering her mouth with her right. And then he was gone. Joan sank against the wall silently sobbing as Annie put her arm around her.

"Get her some water, Bernice," she said.

When Helen returned, Annie explained that they'd be leaving. "Do you want me to come back and help out with the cleanup?"

"No honey, go ahead. I only have to pass on the reigns to the cleanup crew and I'll be right there. Don't forget your things."

The three girls piled into Annie's car and drove out of the lot just as the rain began to fall.

Chapter Thirteen

"Captain Ashenback."

"Yes, Sir?"

"Your work is exemplary."

"Thank you, Sir."

"Yes, if we'd known you were such a stealthy, resourceful individual, we would have found a place for you long ago on this side of things."

"Thank you, Sir."

Harry observed the general from the corner of his eye as the tall man paraded back and forth in front of him. He was congenial, almost flip. Harry's instincts told him that that meant that he was about to be "rewarded."

"Yes, indeed. Now Captain," the general went on, "you may be feeling some degree of fatigue. After all, you have been away from you home and family for some time now." His viewed Harry from the corner of his eyes. "You're a family man, aren't you, Captain Ashenback?"

"Yes, Sir."

"And certainly there are rewards for bravery; medals, commendations, even promotions in some circumstances, as you well know."

"Yes, Sir."

"In fact, your promotion to captain came as a result of your excellent work in Tunisia. You should be proud of that body of work, Captain."

"Yes, Sir."

"Well, good. And in this war, we've seen turnabout. Quite a lot has changed for the Allies since the United States has come in. But it isn't enough. Here, for instance, in Italy, we're just not making the progress we need to make."

Here it comes, thought Harry.

"I have been given the task of relaying certain information by whatever means necessary, to VI Corps. You're familiar with that outfit, aren't you, Captain?"

The general knew full well that he was. He was one of only two covert messengers on assignment between base and VI Corp.

"Yes, Sir."

"Yes. Well, the problem is the Corps is now engaged in some complex maneuvers, and in need of some information, however, at this point in time, that information needs to be conveyed through rather a wide pocket of Nazi occupied territory. Italy may have surrendered, but as you know, Germany has not. They decipher our codes almost as soon as we design them."

The general stood for a long while staring at the ground. Neither man spoke. Then as if he realized he was in a hurry, the general snapped to, and squinted at Harry.

"Captain Ashenback, we would like you to be that conveyor. We will not command it. But we request it. Can you comply with this request?"

"Yes, Sir."

And so, on November 20th in Southern Italy, Harry set out for his 27th solo mission north near the Sangro River, to relay urgent messages via documentation to VI Corp. Harry's vehicle was a first-class Army jeep. Unfortunately, it had been so badly battered and even looked as if it had been fired on, that Harry had been instructed to take along 12 quarts of oil, and to keep a sharp watch on the oil gauge. Apparently, one of the injuries the jeep had sustained was a bullet wound to the base of the oil plug. Once it got going, the jeep dripped oil willy nilly. But because its engine was both oil and air-cooled, the Army had determined that the jeep's condition did not pose a major threat to the conveyor as long as he possessed the necessary skills to replace the oil.

There was quite a bit of necessary replacement oil, as it turned out, but Harry was on top of it. He would have much preferred to fix the hole, but he wasn't given the option.

He had departed the American base at 5:00 a.m. destined for the Sangro River. Hours later and sixty or so miles inside Nazi territory, he had come across neither difficulties nor confrontations of any kind. Harry chuckled remembering the café owner and his wife that morning, insisting that he take with him a sack of food enough to feed an army—at least a very small one.

"I'm only driving one day," he had said. "Do you think I'll need 10 loaves of bread?"

"It'sah no braid," said Mrs. Dulay. "Youah lookah. It's a pepperoni bread, withah cheese. No? And you takah this."

"Yes, it's important," her husband had insisted as she pushed the gallon of sangria into his hands. His English was clearer, and he knew Americans did not feel the same urgency about provisions as the Europeans, who had, and would continue to, suffer hunger and even starvation. "You nevah know, Signor Harry. You don' nevah know."

Harry stashed it all into a second pack. "I'll share it with the guys," he said. "Thanks." As far as the locals knew, he was going South for an R&R.

It was smooth sailing, and while chilly, at least he had no glare from the sun to deal with. But it wasn't long before the rain came. Gently at first, then becoming heavy and suddenly like a frenzied curtain, punching at the jeep. It belted down in waves, blinding Harry to the point where he frantically searched for a place to wait it out on the narrow, winding path. He had never witnessed such fierce rain, and it was coupled with strong, gale force wind. It was more blinding than any snowstorm he could remember. He began to wonder if he were actually still on the road, any road.

It can't last forever, he thought as he finally found a spot to pull over. Maybe I'll just pull up the hood on my pancho and check the oil.

After trying to get into the rhythm of the torrents, he opened the door and made a dash for it, grabbing the oil opener from the back, and splashed around front, popped the hood and saw a fresh slick of oil fully mixing with the pond of water under the jeep. The engine was leaking at a much greater rate than anyone had anticipated, a strong steady drip.

"Good thing I came out to check on you," he said out loud trying to steady his frayed nerves. "You look mighty thirsty."

Back inside the jeep, cold and wet, he was eager to make tracks. But only a few miles later, traveling at a snail's pace, he had no choice but to pull over again. He wasn't sure, but he thought he saw a vehicle well to the rear of him. It could be an Allied vehicle, he knew, but it could also be Nazi. And it could be nothing but his imagination playing tricks on him. Regardless of who it was, at the pace at which he was creeping and with what his oil meter was telling him, he'd best add another can or face the possibility of an engine meltdown. There would be no air cooling in this mess. With another 20 miles to go before getting back into Allied territory, being stranded in a storm did not make for attractive circumstances.

The wind had loosened the canvas flaps at the sides of the jeep, making visibility even more difficult. Harry was sure he'd stopped in a safe spot, but as he stepped out, he barely caught himself from sliding underneath the jeep, skidding into water up to his calves. He grabbed for the door, avoiding the fall, but gouged his wrist on a sharp strip of metal loose on the door frame. The deeply pierced flesh left him woozy. Instinctively he returned to the relative safety of his vehicle. The wound was serious, and bleeding heavily. The kit he had brought contained bandaging and sutures, but with only his left hand to do the work, it would be slow going and awkward. Instead, he managed something of a pressure bandage, and was able to slow the bleeding, but the cloth was still showing red. He pulled it as tightly closed as he could, and restarted the engine.

He moved forward in a kind of jerking manner, as the unrelenting storm pounded on. It was an experience, he told himself, a growth opportunity. He tried to think of funny ways to relate his story to his buddies in an attempt to keep up his spirits.

"I'm actually driving an LCD," he said aloud. "Heck of a way to get a Purple Heart," he nodded, looking at his wrist. "Injury by door frame." Now that's funny, he thought, when suddenly the jeep's front wheels lurched over the edge of roadway that was no longer there.

Captain Ashenbach had no way of knowing that the once seven-foot wide road had become a two-foot road with nothing but a deep cutaway on the left.

He braked hard, trying to get a hold of the road, something, anywhere, grasping the wheel desperately with the left, and then even the wounded right hand. But gravity was winning and as he felt the road fall away entirely, he cradled himself forward, instinctively placing the wounded wrist over his head, and his left wrist over that as the jeep tumbled down the ravine over and over until it came to a stop, twenty feet down and just ten inches above the deep rushing torrent of a swollen creek.

The rain continued, crushing the disabled jeep and passenger deeper into the dirt, more secure, but more embedded. For some time, Harry lay in a dark fog, his wounded wrist throbbing, and his head bleeding at the left temple. But then a loud thunder crash jolted the exposed side of the jeep brought Harry out of his stupor. Semi-conscious, he blinked and felt around for his gun. Locating it, he regained a degree of vision, found the forward position of his jeep, focused, and looked straight into the center of a swastika.

"Happy Thanksgiving!" called Bernice as she put the turkey platter onto Helen's beautifully set table. She looked from one face to the next and shook her head. "Well, I can understand *my* sad mug, with everybody in my family sick, but what's you guys' excuse?"

"I was okay until you said 'Happy Thanksgiving,'" said Annie. "Thanks a lot."

"Well, yeah, that's the idea," teased Bernice. Annie made a face. "Oh, hey, I know things are rough right now with Dick not 100% captured—"

"*Captured!*" cried Joan.

"Well, you know what I mean," Bernice brushed her off. "And Annie hasn't heard from Sylvester in a while—"

"How about 2 weeks again," said Annie. "*Two weeks.*"

"Okay, two weeks, and Helen, well, maybe it's been a while for you too, but—"

Helen slapped her hand on the table. "You know what? She's right. Bernice is 100% right. We do not have any bad news. No, not even you, Joanie. We only have un-news."

Annie chuckled. "Un-news. I like that."

"Would they want us all mopey like this? I don't think so."

"Well Dick might not—" Joan began.

"Dick *especially* would not want you upset," Helen said. "He's so nuts about you, he's all thumbs. I know he didn't propose, but lots of guys don't when they don't know about their future. That could be all it is, Joan. Really and truly."

Joan's face brightened. "Gosh. I never thought of it that way."

"Sure! And like Bernice said, we have no reason to be upset or sad or even worried. We'll know when we know, and unless it's bad, and until we know, we might as well go on and anticipate a beautiful, rosy future. What's the sense in doing anything else at all?"

It was as if the fog cleared and the sky began to lighten. The table became alive with conversation and plans for the following week's bazaar.

"I can't believe how many shell jewelry pieces we've made," said Joan, "and Bernice, your beautiful pictures and figurines. We'll bring in a lot of money for St. Benedicts with those!"

"Not counting the oversized insane bird," Annie chided.

Bernice snorted at her. "How many *do* we have, Helen?" she asked.

"Oh honey, I've lost count. But I know it will cover a whole table and probably more. Let's just hope the browsers like them as much as we do."

"Well, if they don't, I'll be buying them," Annie laughed. "As it is, Helen, I've got my eye on that butterfly set you made."

"Oh, the yellow and blue?" Joan said. "No fair, that's the one *I* like!" she laughed.

"Not the yellow and blue, although that one's pretty, too. I mean the purple and rose, the one that looks like the butterfly's got roses on her wings."

"You're so sweet," said Helen. "I never thought of that. I am planning to buy Bernice's St. Theresa's Garden."

"Oh, that, too!" said Annie. "Fortunately, you did a lot of those, Bernice."

"Yes, great artists must share their talents with others less fortunate," Bernice said.

"I know you're kidding," Annie said, "but your pieces are incredibly creative as well as beautiful."

"They really are," said Joan, grabbing Bernice's hand.

"I say you're both right," said Helen. "Could I please have that gelatin mold, Honey. It looks fabulous!"

"I added celery this time," said Joan, handing it across the table to Helen. "Nuts, sliced pear, celery —
"

"Eggs, olives, pimentos, and red pepper," finished Bernice.

"Ew! No I didn't!" said Joan laughing. "You're looking for a fight."

"Not with food on the table!" said Helen.

"Yeah you ingrates," said Annie, taking a fresh slice of turkey. "But realistically, Helen, how much is Father Bertrand hoping to take in?"

"He is hoping to cover the utility bills and a few other expenses for the next few months, up to Easter," Helen said. "Maybe in the area of $200. And I think he can do it, because remember, there will be tables of baked goods, table coverings, Christmas decorations—"

"What are they making?" Bernice asked.

"I heard a group of women had been decorating candles with beads and paint," Helen continued. "I haven't seen any of them, but I am very interested in looking at those."

"Oh yes!" said Joan. "What else?"

"Well, one of the ladies and her friend from another church are working on nut shells. They paint nativity scenes inside, or arrange dyed cotton wool and tiny slivers of wood to look like the Baby Jesus and paint stars. Those will be beautiful on the little trees some of the households will have."

"Will you put up a tree, Helen?" Bernice said.

"Oh, I don't know. It seems silly without Harry here."

Annie and Joan exchanged glances. "Well we are," said Annie. "Boys or no boys, this is our first

Christmas together and we're making our house as Christmasy as we can."

"So are we," said Bernice.

The girls waited for Helen's response as she played with her pretty Thanksgiving napkin on her lap. "It's not the same, though, is it? You two have moved into your own new home," she said looking at Annie and Joan, "and you're still in your home," she said to Bernice. "I've got a home that was once full of bustle and activity at the holidays, and this year, it's only me."

Joan teared up and Annie fished for a handkerchief for her.

"What about today?" Bernice demanded. "It's Thanksgiving Day. Are you alone?"

Helen was startled by the brusqueness of her voice. "Well...no."

"No," said Bernice more warmly. "Because we're here. We'll never leave you alone, Helen, you ought to know that by now."

Spontaneously the three girls rose to go to Helen and smother her in kisses and hugs.

"Bernice said it right," said Annie. "If you can stand us, we'll be here."

"Yes. Christmas and all," said Joan.

"Christmas?" said Helen, "How ever will you manage that? You've all got families."

"We'll work it out," said Joan. The others nodded.

They ate in silence. Then Joan spoke up.

"Do you think I have piano legs?"

"Piano legs?" said Helen. "What. . .?"

"You got four of them?" Bernice asked, fully stuffing involved.

Annie giggled. "No Joan. You don't have piano legs."

"Because I read that that is one thing men do *not* find attractive."

"Piano legs?" Helen said. "Musical. . .?"

"Did you *show* him your legs?" demanded Bernice.

"No!"

"Then how would he even know if you *had* piano legs?"

"Which she does not. Now onward to the pumpkin pie!"

"What are piano legs?" asked Helen.

Chapter Fourteen

Sylvester grunted for breath, then leaned over the rail and wretched again. Swaying on his legs, he turned and made for the metal benching not two feet behind him and sat down on it hard. He rose and fell with the swells beneath him, then headed for the rail again. Returning to the bench, he caught sight of Bobby's laughing face. He was actually laughing. Here was Sylvester, probably dying of. . . of what? Dying of excessive throwing up? And his buddy was standing there laughing!

"Some pal you turned out to be!"

Bobby stopped laughing, wiped his eyes, and steadied his friend as he handed him a metal cup of something. "Here," he said. "Have that. It's supposed to cure your ills."

"What'll cure my ills, as you put it, is dry land, to be standing on the ground!" Sylvester said with emotion but very little conviction.

"Yeah, yeah, yeah. Drink it and shut up, landlubber."

"What's in it?"

"I really don't know," Bobby said. "I told the Captain's mate you were feeling the swells and he said to give it to you."

"Shit! That's hot!"

"Hot? No it isn't," said Bobby.

Sylvester coughed. "I mean spicy hot," he said. "Like pepper." He coughed again.

"I guess it's some brew they use for seasickness," Bobby said.

Their ship carried a merchant crew. Bobby and Sylvester had hitched a ride, having made it across the tip of Italy, on their mission way up to the northern port of Bari, where they were to interpret witnesses again, in much the same way things had gone in the southern Italian villages.

"If I had known they were going through this kind of weather, I would have waited," Sylvester said.

"Yeah, you would have waited. In the stockade you would have waited. I don't remember actually being asked our opinion on the matter," Bobby said. "Are you sure you don't have a cigarette? It's colder than a—"

"No, I don't smoke," Sylvester said. "Believe it or not. I'm the only one in my family who doesn't. And we volunteered, as you recall. I wouldn't be in the stockade. I'd been in front of a plate of your calamari friti."

"That's some pronunciation," Bobby chided. "Hard to believe you're not a native."

Sylvester chuckled. "Nice to see your spirits picking up, even if it's at my expense."

"Yeah, got good times and bad, I guess," Bobby said, shrugging off his recent period of the blues. "We can take it. We're men."

"What day is it today, anyway? Aren't we due in to Bari?"

"That's what I heard down below," Bobby said. "In fact, they're all down there getting the stuff rigged up to go. I saw some of them carrying up boxes top side, so it must be this morning."

"You know, this stuff worked," Sylvester said, tapping his tin cup. "Thanks Bobby."

"Any time, Buddy," Bobby said smiling. "I got your back."

"Back at ya."

The merchant marines were then rapidly increasing their progress, moving crates astern. "Imah go home today!" shouted one of the men to Bobby. "Lookah, the porta, no?"

"Hey, see, what'd I tell you?" Bobby said to Sylvester. "Sounds great, Rico," he continued. "Buona fortuna!"

"Si, si, si," said the man, smiling. He gave a sympathetic wave to Sylvester, and smiled, and continued rapidly on his way below for more crates.

"What do you think they're carrying, Bobby?" Sylvester said.

"I don't know, and I don't wanna know. This is the merchant marine, after all. It's probably you know, bombs and stuff."

Sylvester laughed. "Spoken like a true college man. Bombs and stuff."

Just then, as Rico reached the top of the steps, they saw him look up, drop his box right where he stood and tear off, rushing at them. "Bajo, a bajo!" he screamed, springing at them and forcing them down toward the bench where they'd just been sitting.

Within seconds, all of the other merchant soldiers were either overboard or below, only Rico remained above board covering the two men with his body.

And the sky opened up.

Sylvester and Bobby could see nothing, but all around them, the world shook and bolted like no waves or sea could do. Their ears were stunned by the brilliance and intensity of the sound blasting, exploding around them. The tiny boat siren, which had engaged just seconds before, blended into the wild sounds of the sky, its warning to no avail. The scream of careening bombs blew loud and blasted across the harbor, just in sight. Explosion after explosion followed.

Sylvester imagined the destruction and grew impatient to do something. Covered by Rico, he found it nearly impossible to move. Surely there was something he and Bobby could do. While still in the midst of trying to formulate a plan, there came a deep thud near enough for Sylvester to smell the hot metal. A split second later, the topside of the merchant ship was in ribbons. Explosion after explosion rocked the ship's remains to and fro.

Sylvester was determined to stay conscious. He knew he had been injured because he could not make a connection with his left leg, but he would survive. He would make it. And he would start by seeing to Rico.

It sounded as if the raid was fading. The German planes had done their damage and disappeared except for the very few that had met with fiery ends

in the Adriatic Sea at the gunnery expertise of the
British and Italian forces inside Bari.

Although Sylvester maintained consciousness as
best he could, he realized suddenly to his horror that
he was no longer on the ship. In fact, the ship was no
longer. He was stranded in the sea, an Italian on his
back, and what looked like an eight-by-ten-foot plank
underneath. How was he floating? He desperately
wanted to check Rico but he dared not risk drowning
him. If he just didn't move but let the waves carry
them, they might both float ashore. For a split second,
he imagined Annie standing at the shore, except it
was the South Jersey shore, and then the image was
gone. Instead, he saw the fire. It was huge and black,
with smoke firing up from it like magma from a live
volcano. He and his makeshift float and whoever else
was with him, were heading straight for it.

"I've got to stay conscious," he croaked out. "Stay
awake, stay alive." As if his training gave him
strength, his legs began to feel the ocean in which
they dangled. He kicked as best he could as he tried
to twist away from the fire. "We're going to the
right," he said, as if giving an order. "Moving
starboard of the fire." And slowly, surely, they did.
Rico had not made a sound but Sylvester thought he
could feel him breathing. But where was Bobby?

I can't think about that now. Get Rico ashore, and
then return for Bobby. He's a smart guy. He might
have made it ahead of us, he thought. His head had
begun to ache, so he lowered it as he paddled,
catching site of his scapular, as it floated on the

surface of the water beside him. "Please give me the strength, Dear Lord," he prayed. "Help me manage this task, deliver this man who has saved my life by protecting me with his own."

It seemed like hours before he was spotted by an American rescue boat. Bundled in scratchy wool blankets and drinking hot coffee that tasted like metal, Sylvester felt as if he were in heaven. In the hours that followed, he learned that Rico had been very severely injured. He had taken shrapnel on his upper right side, which had lodged in his neck and lower skull, as well as his shoulder and back. Sylvester had injured his right leg, a deep gash at the ankle and received burns on his lower torso to which both the presence of Rico's body and the salt water had provided protection and tonic. He was humbled by Rico's instantaneous sacrifice.

Father Bertrand smiled as he closed the cashbox. Two hundred and thirty-seven dollars. It was so much more than he had expected, and over fifty dollars more than he even needed. Now he might be able to contribute to some of the other very needy folks in the parish. He had a list he kept privately. Some had applied for help directly, while other names had come from concerned friends of those who were struggling.

He knelt in front of the statue of Our Lady of Perpetual Help in his hallway. "I prayed for your intercession and you have granted my prayer. Our Lord has given with such generosity," he said, "and I am so grateful. Please continue to intercede for those in need and most especially for our dear Father Kuchesky. Please deliver him from whatever evil has befallen him. And give him the strength to endure through it. Amen."

"Meow," commented a familiar voice.

Father turned to see that Celeste had joined him at the prayer table. He chuckled, and picked up his little companion as he rose to his feet. "Thank you for joining in my prayer," he said. "Let's see what we've got for lunch. We'll be making out a Christmas list today, too. Have you got any friends you'd like to add?"

He set the kitten down on her makeshift bed and went to the counter, where she promptly joined him at floor level, rubbing up against his legs.

"Now, see, you get me in trouble with the women of the parish," he said to her. "You leave these white hairs on my trousers, and tongues will wag." He bent down to remove any stray hairs and she jumped into his arms.

He gave up, poured himself a cup of coffee and sat down to pet the kitten and think. How in the world did we get to be such a generous parish, he wondered. Could it possibly be this awful war? Surely the wrongs men are causing to others, these fascists with such hateful ideals, constitutes evil.

Yet, as evil tries to destroy us, what does it do but uncover the truth and the beauty of the human soul? The devil does not win because for one reason, unlike God, he cannot be in all places at one time. He can

start only so many fires of malice, but the image and
likeness of God in us is victorious.

Look at the sacrifice, the offerings of time and
precious ingredients of the women of the parish,
baking, decorating, creating, all for the benefit of
their church and for me—for us, he corrected, smiling
at the kitten. He did not remember the free flow of
services being as common before the heavy strain of
this war. When these people had more, they gave
less. Now that they have less, they are giving more.
And the parishioners, attending the bazaar, making it
such a success—surely that is the hand of God. And
the beauty of the human soul in the face of such
danger and pain.

He recalled his visit with young Bernice and
thought what an admirable young lady she was. He
remembered her request concerning a neighbor that
she felt was in need. How had she put it? Something
like, "she's scraping the bottom of the barrel." He
tapped the tabletop lightly with his pen. Maybe I'll
write out some names on the envelopes so I don't
forget Bernice's friend, Rose. No time like the
present.

But Celeste had gone to sleep purring. As Father
pet her long-haired little head. He hated to wake her,
although he was quite ready for lunch. "Twelve-
forty," he said out loud. "All right, Kitty on the Keys,
I'll give you another twenty minutes while I say my
rosary."

She curled up, making her body into the shape of
an O and continued sleeping.

"Okay, gals, this is it. Let's get these gifts done."

"Golly, Helen, you don't give a kid a break, do you?"

"What do you mean, Bernice?"

"Well, we just finished the bazaar last week, and I think it was a success, too, by the way."

"I heard that all of the breads and baked goods sold," said Joan, "and even most of our jewelry. I'd say it was a raging success!"

"And Bernice's creations went. In fact, two of them before anybody even looked at the jewelry," Annie added.

"It was genius on the part of the other girls to put Bernice's plaques with the decorations. That's really where they belonged," said Helen. "But," she nudged Bernice, "they would have gone anyway."

"Yeah, yeah," said Bernice.

"You can poo poo them all you want, Bernice," said Annie. "But Helen's right. They were the talk of the bazaar. Now you're on the hook for next year, no matter what."

Helen and Bernice exchanged glances then quickly looked away.

"What?" Joan asked, laughing, "have you retired from your new career already, Bernice?"

Bernice laughed. "Great art can't be forced," she said.

"Oh brother," said Annie.

"Do you know if we reached the goal?" Joan asked Helen. "It sure seemed like it."

"You mean financially? Yes, I heard it was more than two hundred dollars, and Father was so grateful. He has a long list you know, of folks in need, and he, well, let's just say I've heard that some needy folks receive anonymous envelopes from the church around this time of year."

"Oh, that's wonderful," said Joan. "I knew he was like that."

"It really is," said Bernice. "Imagine if you were struggling so badly you couldn't find the means to have a Christmas dinner, and along comes an envelope with enough to buy everything you need and then some."

"And for those who are on their own," Helen added, "don't forget, he's got the parish hall opened up. Two of the gals will be hostessing a Christmas night feast."

Everyone fell to quietly taking it in and imagining the older parishioners and those out of work joining together for the holiday, all at the hands of a generous priest and his parish.

"It really makes me feel good, in spite of how things are going with Dick," said Joan.

"How *are* things going?" asked Bernice. "You never tell me anything."

"I'm sorry, Bernice. I just whine about it all the time. Poor Annie's sick of hearing it."

"No I'm not," said Annie. "It keeps my mind off that disappearing man of mine."

"And his floozie," said Bernice.

"Yeah, and his floozie," Annie said.

"Well, Laureen and I both heard from them," Joan began. "And it's wonderful news, at least for now. Neither one is going overseas."

"I bet that's not wonderful news to them, though," said Annie. "Sylvester said if he was going to fight a war, he wanted to fight a war."

"I wouldn't be surprised if they have the same attitude," Helen said. "But the women folk don't feel the same, I bet."

"We sure don't!" said Joan. "Laureen can't believe it. She has been to Mass every day since she heard, I think!"

Everyone laughed.

"Good for her," said Helen.

"So what's the bad news?" said Bernice.

"Well, I got a letter from Dick," Joan said, "but it was more like a written report for civics class or something."

"What?"

"I'm serious."

"Read her that paragraph at the end," Annie said. "This should give you some idea."

Joan got the letter from her purse. "Okay. It goes: Well, I guess I'd better ease on out of here. I have heard that it's best to stay just a little ahead of the schedule, anticipate what they want done and do it. In my situation here, that means conduct a rifle inspection. As the gunnery instructor and sergeant in charge of arms maintenance in this unit, I need to remain alert to all possible troubles. So I'll sign off. Yours truly, Dick Thimble."

Joan looked at Bernice, smirking. "See what I mean?"

Bernice's expression betrayed confusion. She looked at Helen before answering. Helen's face gave nothing away. "Well," she began, "I guess I see. . . "

"You don't sound very sure," said Annie.

"Joanie," said Bernice, "does he seem at all shy to you?"

"No, I wouldn't say shy," said Joan.

"Well, I mean, does he take your hand freely or fling an arm around you, or does it seem more measured and sort of hesitant?"

"Hmm," said Joan. "Gosh, I don't know. Maybe he is like that, come to think of it."

Helen smiled. "So he probably is a little shy, hmm?"

"Yes, I suppose so," said Joan. "In that way, but he talks easily enough."

"What are you guys getting at?" Annie asked. "I thought it was just a guy thing, you know, talk about engines and gasoline and stuff."

"He didn't talk about engines and gasoline!" said Bernice.

"Well, generally," said Annie.

"Oh brother," said Bernice.

"Wait, Bernice, really, what do you mean? I'm curious," said Joan

"Helen?" Bernice asked.

"I think I know what you're getting at," said Helen. "Honey," she said turning to Joan. "re-read that paragraph and think of yourself as the "they" in it, and try to imagine what he might be trying to say without saying it."

"Okay." She read, "Well, I guess I'd better ease on out of here. I have heard that it's best to stay just a little ahead of the schedule, anticipate what *they*, meaning me, Joan, want done and do it. In my situation here, that means conduct a rifle inspection. A *rifle inspection?*"

"Keep going, Joanie," Bernice said.

"As the gunnery instructor and sergeant in charge of arms maintenance in this unit, I need to remain alert to all possible troubles. So I'll sign off. Yours truly, Dick Thimble. Okay, he says he needs to anticipate what I might want. But why would I want a rifle inspection?"

"That's the vehicle! Didn't you take English class in high school?" Bernice said impatiently.

"Bernice," said Helen reproachfully. "Yes, Joan, that's how I see it, too. If you just substitute rifle inspection with proposal of marriage, does that change the meaning? All of what he's saying is true, but he's also seeking some kind of sign, or inclination on your part. Why don't you write him back in kind, telling him that you feel the rifle inspection is called for, even though you are not the sergeant in charge. Just an interested civilian. If we are wrong, then nothing happens. He has not been cornered, and you haven't put yourself out on a limb. "On the other hand, if we are right, then you've indicated that you are interested and that he should go ahead and contemplate the proposal, aka rifle inspection."

"Oh it can't be that intricate!" Annie cried. "Surely he's not that complicated. If he is, poor Joanie! How will you ever communicate with him?"

"I don't know," smiled Joan. "It might be a lot of fun. Of course, I'd have to learn about the parts of a rifle."

Everybody laughed.

"That's the spirit, Joan!" said Helen. "And to be truthful, I don't think even *he* knows that he's done this, a lot of times these shy guys do this stuff kind of subconsciously."

"Whatever you say," Annie said. "Cheesey Pete, Bernice. I had no idea how deep you were."

"I'm not just another pretty face, Annie."

"Okay, now that we've got that solved, we'd better get cracking," said Helen. "We've got exactly 3 hours before vespers."

"I am working on something that can't be seen by some of the eyes here," said Annie.

"So am I," said Joan.

"No problem," Helen said. "Just pick a secret corner of the room and work away."

Two weeks after the raid on Bari, Sylvester was able to hobble with assistance. The injured had been treated in various places, including the private homes of doctors. There was no organized American presence just then, so the citizens of Bari, and the English and Canadian armies rallied. He was fortunate to have received the best available care and he was in much better shape than he had expected to be. But on his mind dwelt the grinding pain of worrying about Bobby, who seemed to have disappeared completely. The thought of his succumbing to the black waters at the harbor stabbed at Sylvester, though he rejected those thoughts, sure within his spirit that Bobby was no such casualty. But where was he?

One emotional fire he could not quell was the deep need to give thanks to and for the heroic actions of Rico Santolossi. He had heard that Rico had not regained consciousness, but that he was alive and being fastidiously cared for by the nuns at Santo Vincenzo's Hospital. He found Rico swaddled in white linen and blankets and freshly bandaged. An elderly nun sat by his bedside reading.

"*Bongiorno*," he said. "I have come to see Rico. *Come 'sta?*"

The nun smiled and slowly rose, closing her book. She took Sylvester's extended hand and nodded. It was clear to her that this American soldier was interested in the welfare of the wounded warrior in her care, and that pleased her. She placed her hands under her chin, tilted her head, and closed her eyes, to show Sylvester that Rico remained unconscious. But she lifted the sheets to reveal that he was heavily bandaged, and his head was badly swollen. Should have been my hard head, Sylvester thought, shaking his head slowly. Sister replaced the cover, and as if reading his mind, she embraced Sylvester. "*Non te preocuparte*," she said. "*Sta bene. Vincenzo, Santo Vincenzo dice sta bene.*"

Sylvester was so overcome at the kindness of the gentle woman and her comforting him, that his heart opened and he cried for the first time in many years. He cried for gratitude, for sorrow, and for the pain surely to come. But standing there in the arms of the elderly nun, he felt safety in the hand of God. And he dug in his spiritual heels, resolving then and there that the terrors of these evil deeds of war would not haunt him, nor anyone else that he could reach.

Chapter Fifteen

"Oh!" said Helen. She woke with a start. "I overslept. What's going on with that alarm clock anyway?"

She rushed through brushing her teeth and getting dressed and still made it to Mass by 6:45 am.

"Hello, Mrs. Ashenbach," whispered Laureen, as they both headed inside the church.

"Oh hello, Honey," said Helen. "How are you doing?"

"Just fine!" said Laureen. "Have a nice week!"

"You, too," said Helen. She found a seat near the front of the church on the side closest to the statue of Our Lady of Grace. It was such a beautiful statue. Its mere presence brought comfort to Helen. She wondered who would be attending. Would the girls be there? Annie usually slept late, or at least later than the others, but she thought she might see Bernice or Joan. Dear Bernice, she thought. She wondered how Bernice would tell the other girls, and when. It was her secret to tell, after all, but it did seem as if Bernice were plodding along. If it were me, Helen thought, I'd have come right out with it.

Just as the Mass started, Helen spotted not Bernice, not Joan, but Annie sitting up front across the aisle. Annie had not spotted her. She was deep in her own thoughts. It's awfully early for her, Helen thought. I wonder if the same angel woke her that got me up instead of my alarm clock.

After Mass, Helen tapped Annie on the shoulder. Annie looked up, startled. Her eyes looked swollen to Helen and her expression nowhere near as merry as her usual self.

They decided to stop in at the coffee shop on 23rd and Jersey. It was raining cold and hard, and just warm enough for it not to be snow. Helen drove.

"It's so good to get out of the rain!" Annie said, settling into the booth and taking off her rain hat. "I miss the trolley in the city, but not today I don't!"

"This place is so cozy," Helen said. She'd taken her umbrella, but only a small cap protected her hair and it was rain sprinkled. "I think I'm giving up umbrellas. Look how wet my head is!"

Annie smiled.

"You okay, Honey?" Helen asked.

"I am, but I'm not," Annie said. "I woke up very oddly this morning, and early, if you couldn't tell."

"That did surprise me," Helen admitted. "What do you mean, 'oddly'?"

Annie looked around the room, searching for the words. "I felt some kind of danger, some kind of fear, I guess you could say. It wasn't a dream. It was just a . . . feeling?" she finished, as if asking a question.

Helen stared at her. "Fear about what?" she asked slowly.

Annie stared back. "Sylvester."

"Annie, I don't want to alarm you, but I think you and I were meant to see each other today because I had the same startling feeling. It woke me up. Or something did. . ."

Annie took a deep breath and sighed. "What do you think it means? What is it all about?" The normally jolly Annie who had no problem covering her feelings seemed near the breaking point.

"I won't lie to you, Annie," Helen said. "I'm scared. I don't know what it means. I have never felt this way before. But we've done the best thing we could by praying this morning, attending Mass."

"I know," said Annie sighing.

"You know if I get out of bed at 6 am and come out into a rain storm to be . . ." her voice trailed off.

"These things we do," Helen said, "the bazaar, dances, caring for the men that *are* here, they really kind of carry us, keep us happily or at least distractedly occupied. It's like a salve. But some mornings—or nights—the salve doesn't work, and it's then that we're forced to face. . . everything."

Annie nodded slowly. "Yeah. Sometimes I just want to give up being grown and run away home."

Helen smiled.

"Just coffee?" asked the waitress.

"No," said Helen, suddenly resolute. "We're going to have eggs. And toast, too." She tapped the table for emphasis. "My treat."

"And waffles?" said Annie.

"And *waffles*."

It was daylight again, and not as cold. Harry was grateful for the cold on the one hand; he had read that it could slow bleeding and even infection. He could still feel all of his limbs. On the other hand, it wasn't a pleasant sensation. As much as possible, he stayed bundled up in his makeshift canvas hut.

He peered out into the desolate terrain. How long had it been, anyway? He shook his head, catching sight of the swastika that had long since ceased to terrorize him. When in the world were the Nazis going to come for their tank? Were they so well equipped that they could afford to just leave heavy equipment in the field, abandoned and unattended? He wanted like the dickens to do something to efface that evil swastika staring him in the eyeball every time he stuck his head out of the jeep.

"He had made it a point to close his eyes each time he ventured out to use his makeshift latrine. Once the rain had stopped and the river below subsided, it turned back into the small creek it had been, and Harry was grateful for the water. After all, a gallon of sangria could go only so far.

"However, he was even more grateful on these cold days, for the huge loaves of bread, tucked in generously with pepperoni slices and mozzarella cheese. He remembered refusing them, and by the grace of God, the restaurateur's wife had insisted. It may not be a varied set of rations he allowed himself, but it was hearty and contained enough to keep him functional and alert.

Harry checked for his secret document. It was in place. How long had it been since his dispatch to VI Corps? He was certain his failure would be met with reprimand. He'd gone over and over in his mind how he had come to drive off the roadway. But he could come to only one conclusion; driver error. He must have become disoriented, maybe from the shock of the cut.

And oh, it had been a deep one! He had thanked God daily for having brought his field kit and for having somehow the dexterity and fortitude in that first night to stitch his own wrist, left-handed. It wasn't a pretty job, but he had closed the wound and the blood flow had slowed, then stopped.

Helen would be sick to see it, he thought. Helen. But instantly he toughened. No, he could not afford to think of her now.

First weakness and pain, and then the wind and cold had kept him from it, but maybe today, he thought, I could hike up that hill and figure out how I managed to destroy an Army jeep and any chance of getting this code through to VI Corps.

After work that day, Joan went into the kitchen to figure out dinner. I've got some leftovers in here, she thought, sustering through the refrigerator. Out loud, she said, "Annie sure keeps this refrigerator clean. I never clean it. I hope she doesn't think I'm some kind of slob."

"She doesn't," Annie said from the living room.

Joan jumped, bumping her head on the refrigerator ceiling. "Ouch! Hey!"

"Ouch, hey?"

Joan giggled. "Yeah. Ouch, comma, hey. And where did you come from? Your shop is still open."

"I let Margaret watch it for me. She loves to fill in for me and I just had to. . . I don't know."

Joan closed the refrigerator and went in to sit next to Annie. "What's wrong?" she asked.

Annie shook her head. "Nothing," she said. "It's just a feeling—I can't explain it. Just, I know we've been through dry periods like this, when he can't write me, but this time, I don't know, Joanie. It feels different. And the funny thing is Helen has the same feeling."

"Helen has the same feeling about Sylvester?"

Annie giggled in spite of herself. "No! About Harry."

"Oh."

"I guess you noticed I got up well before dawn today."

"I did. I thought you wanted to make Mass."

"Oh I did, but Joan, I got up at 6:00 in the morning! Where's that playing?"

"I see what you mean. You didn't set your alarm clock then?"

"No, I just woke up, and I woke up thinking Sylvester was in trouble, or pain or. . . something."

"It makes sense, Annie. Some people are just so close that they can feel each other's feelings. You and he must be one of those couples."

"But what do you think it means? Helen thinks that Harry's in trouble, too."

"Oh boy," said Joan sighing and leaning back. "I hope you two are both wrong and maybe just overtaxed with the burden of not hearing from them for so long."

"From your lips to God's ears," Annie said. "Speaking of hearing from, you got a letter today. I put it on the table there."

"Oh! How did I miss *that?*" Joan brightened, grabbed the letter and opened it on the spot.

"I'll give you some privacy," Annie said. "You want some tea?"

"Love some," said Joan. She opened Dick's letter.

> *It was very pleasant to hear from you, a tender voice in the midst of all of this mania and scheduling and technical instruction. The departures and arrivals are coming so rapidly now, I can't remember who's arriving and who's going. I only hope I've helped to prepare these young men. They're only 18 years old, most of them. It's as if I'm training my little brother, and that seems not only ridiculous but outright wrong. I train them to go off to fight a war I'm thoroughly shielded from. By them. But enough of that talk. I was happy to hear that you got my last letter, and all of your thoughts on the things I'm working on here. I was thinking we were going to do that rifle inspection, and I guess so were you, but we ended up not having it at all! That surprised most of the fellows, who were all ready and everything. I guess in war times, you never know what's coming next.*

"Great," Joan said.

"What? Here's your tea."

"Mmh, smells good. Thanks. He says they cancelled the rifle inspection or they didn't have it in any case."

"Oh yeah, the rifle inspection . . . Well, what does that mean?"

"I don't know," said Joan thoughtfully. "I don't know if the vehicle is still out there or back in the garage."

"What?" laughed Annie.

"I'm just trying to think along the lines of what Bernice was saying," Joan said. "Use the rifle inspection the way he intended. So I said I thought he should anticipate it and be ready."

"Oh, well that's good," said Annie.

"Yeah, but now he says they never had it. What in the world does that mean?"

Annie stared at her. "You better ask Bernice," she said finally.

The church was still chilly. The rain just might turn to snow, Bernice thought. I am glad I don't have to take the streetcar in. Bitsy was up in the choir loft working through the parts, practicing with another soloist. Bernice had practiced her own solo and it was clean as a whistle. She had always loved to sing, but how will it be to sing a solo, she wondered. What does it feel like while you're doing it? It's a year of new adventures, she thought.

Carol stepped into the back of the church just then, and stood shaking off her rain hat. She saw Bernice and smiled. "It's raw out there!"

"That's the word for it," Bernice said. "They say it might turn to snow."

"Oh that would be nice!" Carol said. "I love snow."

"Me, too."

Then a quietness descended on them as they listened through the floor to the soloist upstairs and then Bitsy stopping her and then giving instructions as only Bitsy could do. Bernice giggled a little. Carol smiled and quickly turned away. Bernice thought she saw her expression change a split second before she turned.

Suddenly, a dagger hit Bernice. Right in the heart. For an instant, she froze, suspended in a sea of her own guilt. When she turned back to Carol, she had disappeared up the stairs to the loft. "Carol!" she whispered, so as not to disturb the rehearsal as she ascended the stairs behind her. But Carol had quickly found a spot and was seemingly, merrily getting out her music.

Bernice watched her for a moment, and then sat down where she stood, slowly taking out her own music. How in the world did I get into this, she wondered.

"No, the second stanza, yes, that's it. Okay, start again," said Bitsy, her voice growing impatient. Bernice winced for the soloist.

After rehearsal, Bernice stayed behind, letting the others leave while she helped collect the music and set it on top of the bookcase.

"Sounding pretty good," said Bitsy. "You're going to knock 'em dead on Christmas Eve. They'll wonder where in the world you came from!"

"Well, as nice as that is to hear, Bitsy—"

Bitsy stood up and held up her hand. "I know," she said. "I've been hard on you."

"Not so much hard on me—"

"I know, I can be very nasty, very demanding."

"Listen, Bitsy, I don't want to do the solo."

Bitsy sighed and approached Bernice, sat down beside her and leaned in as she spoke. "I know I'm difficult to work with. I am. But the only reason I act this way is because I want to get the best sound, the best performance. I know what kind of talent I am working with here and I want to get the best out of each individual. I sincerely want that, nothing more."

Bernice looked at her calmly. "I know. And I'm glad you brought that up because it really does concern me. To be honest, Bitsy, the soloists have the same desire you have, to do their absolute best. But I think some of them, the younger ones in particular, do exactly the opposite under. . . pressure. I think a few words of encouragement might go a long way."

"I'll do it," said Bitsy, standing up with a smile. "So will you please do the solo?"

"Well, no," said Bernice, not aware of how funny her answered sounded, being still adrift in thoughts of Carol's feelings.

Bitsy laughed and trotted off down the stairs. "Oh you kids," she said, "always joking around."

Bernice listened to her voice echoing down the hall as she left. She gathered her things and decided it was time for a heart to heart.

Joan's heart beat frantically as she took the pen in hand. She wiped off the tip. This will be the time it will decide to leak out all over this pretty stationery, she thought. I should just write in pencil.

But there was something much more elegant about using a pen. Joan's handwriting had won awards in second grade, and by the time she entered young adulthood, it was truly masterful. Nothing but ink would bring its swirling beauty fully to life. She started the letter, December 19, 1943. She put down her pen looked at the date. The 19th already! It seemed like yesterday they had all attended the bazaar, but it had been almost 2 weeks. She had been so proud of her shell creations. Every single one had sold, and brought in over $20 altogether. She had been very secure in the thought that jewelry for her friends would be just as well received on Christmas.

Safely tucked away in her bedroom was the pair of red and white earrings she'd made Annie. With her dark hair, Joan thought, those earrings will look so merry at Christmas, and then any time after . . . well never mind that, she said shaking away dark thoughts. To go with it, she had made a red and white brooch in the shape of a heart. For Bernice, she had used purple and white, and made her a brooch in the shape of a cross. She didn't know why she'd done that, but something had inspired her and it had come out quite nicely. At the intersection, she'd made a tiny white rose. It was fun trying to visualize spunky Bernice wearing her purple earrings, but especially her rose studded cross, just being Bernice. And for Helen, she had made lush yellow roses with green stems—both a pin for her lapel, and a pair of earrings. The earrings didn't have stems and were rounded, made of deep yellow and white petals. The yellow color was warm and welcoming, Joan had felt, just like Helen.

"Mom would love a pair of those, too," Joan said out loud. "I should write that down and work on it tomorrow with the girls." She smiled. Despite the frustration and difficulties of the war and the not knowing about so many things, the Christmas season carried some semblance of merry because of her dear friends. We all have struggles, she thought, but somehow sharing them makes them manageable.

She picked up her pen again. *Dear Dick,* she wrote, *It was wonderful to hear from you. I don't know very much about the workings of the military, but it sounds as if you have everything in your watch well in hand. I trust that whatever decisions you make will be the right ones.*

Joan smiled. Bernice will like that, she thought.

Bernice knelt. It seemed that the eyes in the statue of Mary were especially sympathetic that afternoon and looking directly at her; that her arms were embracing Bernice as they never had before. "How could I have been so selfish?" Bernice whispered.

"How could I have put my own sense of importance and glory, above the feelings of someone else?" She was remorseful but not tearful. "I don't feel sorry for myself, I feel sorry for Carol, and I would feel sorry for letting Bitsy down—if she had the slightest idea I was doing that, thought Bernice.

There's no other way to do it than to fake a sore throat. I'll sing with the choir but from the pew here, and I'll sit with Annie and them, so I can still sing, my scheme undetected. She raised her eyes to the Blessed Mother again and it seemed that Mary was saying, "Good thinking!" Bernice almost giggled as she left the church.

Chapter Sixteen

"Your name, Sir?"

Harry jerked around, his head narrowly missing the butt of the rifle pointed at him. It was an English-sounding voice, and it spoke in English, but as the man attached to it stood right beside the enormous Nazi tank, Harry was distinctly uneasy.

"Sergeant Harold Ashenbach," he said, "United States Army." He began to recite his serial number, but the man lowered his rifle and waved his hand.

"We *thought* you were Yankee," he said, "but mixed up here with this tank, just wanted to make sure."

Well, thought Harry, that was like living my life to the end and back in four seconds.

"I can't tell you how relieved I am to hear the English language," said Harry. He put out his hand. "Harry Ashenbach."

"Ford Blankenship, lieutenant, Royal Canadian Army. We've heard of you."

"Pleased to meet you," said Harry. "You're kind of out of your way here, aren't you? Isn't this Nazi territory?"

"*Was*," said Blankenship. "They've retreated again, up the hills, with us and you fellows hot at their heels. We're part of the clean-up crew."

Harry whistled. "I don't think I can tell you how relieved I am to hear that! It's been a very long few days."

"Few days?" Blankenship said. "If you're the Ashenbach who went missing a while back, it's been more like a few weeks."

"Weeks!"

"Weeks. You probably don't remember half of it."

As Harry stood trying to reconcile the phantom time, Blankenship noticed the rugged stitching on his wrist.

"Is there someone else here? You got someone with you?"

"No. Solo mission."

"Then. . . you did that?" he asked, indicating Harry's repair work.

"Oh. Yes. Messy work, but it did the trick."

"You stitched your own wrist. Your own *right* wrist?" Blankenship was incredulous. "No wonder they sent *you*!"

Harry snorted. "What have you come across, I mean in your capacity as cleanup? Have you picked up many?"

"So far, a few nice caches of wine is about all we've found, other than this old abandoned clunker." He kicked the base of the tank. "I wouldn't put a man in one of those no matter what."

"No? I was under the impression that the Germans had some pretty superior quality tanks," said Harry.

"Ay, they do. But this model went out with the cave men. The whole front under panels might as well be made out of paper. If you hit it just at the right angle, you can blast that baby like a jelly doughnut. If you get a shot through the gunnery, it can bounce around in there like popcorn. Not a great place to be."

Harry chuckled at the visual. "Sounds a little vulnerable."

"Yeah, a bit!"

The two men were joined by a second man.

"So are you planning to spend the rest of your time out here?" he said to Harry, smiling. "Or can we drop you somewhere."

"I'm pretty sure I should put in an appearance," said Harry. "I'm with the maintenance commission, and I guess they'd be happy to have my services up at VI Corps."

"VI Corps, okay. You let us know where to go. To tell you the truth, when we saw that deep gully, we didn't expect to see any survivors down here. I'm sure they've given up on you."

"Deep gulley? What do you mean?"

"Isn't that where you got knocked off the road up there?" Blankenship pointed to where Harry's jeep had begun its tumble down the hill. "Didn't you see the cut out there? It's a common trick. These guys, if they don't have any mines, on retreat, they cut out places in the road so night time traveling is treacherous. Were you coming through at night?"

"It was in a rain storm at night—"

"Rain storm?" interrupted Blankenship. "You mean that storm back on the 2nd?"

"Yeah, that's the day I started out."

"Well, it *is* a shocker you're still alive. They said that river was halfway up this hill."

"It was," said Harry.

The lieutenant shook his head. "And with that mess on your wrist, and looks like you got knocked on the forehead, too, how on earth did you survive?"

"I guess it was just all in the plan," Harry said. "Well, at least I've got an explanation for my tardiness, now!"

The men laughed as they gathered to turn Harry's jeep and tow it up the gulley. "We'll tow her in," said Blankenship. "She's going to need some work, it looks like."

"I'd say so," said Harry. "Give me just a second and I'll pop in the back." He gathered the secret documents and stuffed them in his waist, and grabbed the St. Christopher medal dangling from what had been his makeshift tent, bowed his head in thanks, and rejoined the others."

The morning of December 20th dawned relatively calmly in Abbotsville, the temperature having dropped to 18 degrees and a soft blanket of snow collected at the base of the sidewalks and streets. Cars drove more slowly, and, from a purely visual perspective, it was a lovely day. But Annie did not feel lovely. What had gnawed at her the day before was now waging open warfare. Her breath came shorter and her appetite was altogether absent.

"You're up again?" Joan called from the bathroom. "Are you all right?"

"Hi Joanie," she said miserably. "Yeah, I'm all right." Annie sat slumped on the couch, a magazine she wasn't reading beside her with the low lamp on. She pulled her thick terrycloth robe around herself.

Joan joined her. "What can I do?"

Annie shook her head. "I know when things get to you like this you're supposed to do for other people, but I can't seem to do anything, Joan. I feel almost paralyzed."

Joan hugged her. "I'm so sorry. How long has it been now since you heard from him?"

Annie stood up and exhaled, pacing the length of the couch. "I don't really know. More than 2 weeks. I think 3 or maybe 4. I can't even remember, I don't want to know."

"If it were bad news, I'm sure his mom would have told you," Joan said. "I don't want to even mention that possibility, but she would never let you sit and wonder. Never." Joan felt her eyes welling up at the thought. How in the world could Annie stand it, she wondered?

"I only met her the one time at the coffee shop just before he left," Annie said. "But he's been writing to her as well, I'm sure."

They both gazed at their Christmas tree in the dim light. It was a tree of hope. Its tiny branches were reassuring, embracing arms.

"I'm glad we got those lights," Joan said.

"Your father is a wonderful man," said Annie, and then she began to cry.

"Sylvester is a wonderful man, too," Joan said becoming strong for her friend. "*Is*, not *was*. He's alive and well. I'm very tuned into these things, I would know. Mom says I'm psychotic."

Annie stopped crying and burst out laughing. "*Psychic*," she said, "like you pick up on things. Not psy*chotic*, like you're insane." She wiped her eyes. "Bernice is rubbing off on you."

"Oh!" Joan said, joining in the laughter. "I guess I get mixed up sometimes. What would you do without my inanity to make you laugh?" she said, punching Annie on the shoulder.

"I don't know," Annie said sighing. "I'm just glad for it."

Just a little ways away, Helen's morning was similarly foggy. "I've gotten no news," she said aloud as she gathered the trash into the kitchen trashcan, "so there's no reason to be upset. Unless I know something for sure, just go on with my business."

She sat down and sighed. It was no use. She knew something was wrong. It was clear as the "nose in your face," as Joan would say. She chuckled in spite of herself. She could hear Annie correcting, "Nose *on* your face, *on* your face. It can't possibly be in your face, and if it was, it wouldn't be very clear!"

Okay, okay, she told herself, be thankful for small blessings, even if they are just the imaginings of things that could happen. And the snow. It's just beautiful. A slice of heaven! Oh! No, not a slice of heaven, not yet!

Just as she stood up, the doorbell rang, and she froze in her tracks. It was 8:15 in the morning. Who else would ring the doorbell at 8:15 in the morning? Her heart pounded like a bowling ball slamming against the inside of her body as she moved forward on progressively numbing legs the very few steps to the door. Through the peephole, she saw blue, telegram office, Western Union blue. "Oh dear God," she whispered. "Oh sweet Jesus."

The delivery officer was solemn as he handed her the pen. She signed, took the telegram, and retreated into the safety of her home. She took several deep breaths before walking gingerly to the couch and sitting. She tapped the telegram, Please don't let it be so, she prayed. Please don't let it be so. St. Benedict, St. Joseph, Blessed Mother, please don't let it be so.

She opened the telegram, her eyes bleary, and read its one line message.

"The Army regrets Captain Harry Ashenback, Missing in Action."

"Oh," she said. Her heart was crushing her breathing. She captured little gulps of air as she tried to steady herself. "Missing. Oh dear God." It was too soon. They had so much more left to do, to share. It just wasn't possible. It couldn't be so. She sighed heavily through the mist of tears and despair. She rose from the couch. Almost mechanically, she gravitated toward the place that had meant comfort so many times.

She knelt before the statue of the Holy Family, all decorated for Christmas. Missing doesn't mean *killed*. The thought came to her calmly. There was still hope. Her tears fell to the soft blue rug like snowflakes.

Father Bertrand hung up the telephone. Any other time, the honor of receiving a phone call from the Cardinal would have made his day. The words, however, rang in his ears. Gone to God. The dear friend who had single-handedly instituted the beautiful chaplet there at St. Benedict's Church had been killed, apparently killed, the Cardinal had said—along with other priests and religious that had been housed secretly in a Czech official's private home. The Czech and his family had all been slaughtered. The Nazi soldiers had spared no one, not even the family pet. It had been a gruesome scene of systematic murder.

Such an evil deed, thought Father Bertrand. How could human beings behave in such a manner? Didn't even a thread of humanity exist within their souls?

Again, the word "apparently." *Apparently* because all of the Catholics assassinated in the dwelling had been buried en masse by the Nazis, giving no information, no specifics to anyone. The whole massacre had become known only because of two horrified children found hiding in a shed the next day. The families nearby were aware of the heroics of the slain official, and from that, they were able to piece together those who had been given refuge.

Father knelt solemnly before the crucifix. "I know You have a plan for each of us, and that all things will happen in Your own time, but please, Dear God, if it be possible, please allow my friend, Alphonse, to somehow have survived this horrible tragedy, this very ugly turn of events. I know You are merciful. I trust in You. But if it is so, I pray for his blessed soul."

On Annie's insistence, Joan had left for work. She caught the early bus and with the snow coming down, it was a much better idea to set out early than to slip and slide down the sidewalk later.

On any other day, Annie would have been happy to do just that. She thought of Joan and her loving heart, as big as the ocean, always open to her, never failing. Joan had become so important to Annie, especially since they'd begun to share the little house.

Little by little, they'd gone past sharing only things in common and progressed to being able to sense when the other was feeling particularly at loose ends. Annie thought of the letters Joan had received from Dick. If she had received those letters, she would have pegged him as a good friend, not a romance. But yet, she would never have said such a thing to Joan. And to their credit, they'd shared the contents of those letters with Bernice and Helen.

Bernice! Now there was a shocker. How had she become so deep, so perceptive? Helen, yes, with her years and experience in life, but Bernice. . . what was happening with her? It seemed like as much as she had changed, she was still the same.

And somehow Bernice and Helen had become closer in recent months. That was a good thing, and it made Annie happy in the sense that she felt sorry that things between Bernice and Henry seemed to have faded. Yet maybe she was the only one who felt sorry. Bernice seemed happier than she had ever been. That was probably due to Helen.

Helen was magnificent. And yet the day before, oh she hated to see Helen feeling poorly. Annie shook her head. I've got to give her a call and see if she's feeling any better, she decided. She stood up and put her hand on the telephone just as it rang. She pulled back her hand and laughed out loud. I bet that's Helen and she and I are getting "psychotic" too.

"Hello?"

"Hello, is this Anne diRosa?" a female voice asked.

Annie stood up straight. "Yes."

"Hello, Honey," the voice said, "this is Mrs. Bapini. How are you?"

"Oh, hello Mrs. Bapini," Annie said tentatively. "I'm doing well thank you. And you?"

"Well, Honey. . ." her voice trailed off.

Annie gripped the phone tightly. She thought she heard Mrs. Bapini take a breath. "Are you all right, Mrs. Bapini?"

"No, sweetie," she said. "I'm so sorry to have to call you this way." She sniffed. "But I wanted you to know as soon as possible. The more prayers the better."

"Oh no!" said Annie in a panic. "Sylvester! What's happened?"

"He's missing," Sylvester's mother said, her voice breaking. "I got a telegram. All it said is he's missing in action." She was crying freely then. "He wasn't supposed to be in the action, he was just supposed to be translating. I don't know what happened or where or anything."

Annie's heart went out to her in spite of her own grief. "Missing, though. That's not so bad, Mrs. Bapini. I mean it's plenty bad, but hey, you know Sylvester. He's, he's a really resourceful guy."

"Uh huh," said Mrs. Bapini, wiping her nose. "God bless you, you're right. You're exactly right."

"We gotta be strong," said Annie, both the North Jersey accent and resolve fiercely taking hold. "We gotta hold down the fort, not get worried or nothin' 'cause he's really brave. Right? You hear me?"

"Yes, yes," she answered. "You're right, sweetheart. God will watch over him."

"And his Guardian Angel. Don't forget his Guardian Angel."

"And his Guardian Angel."

There was a long pause. Annie's heartbeat began to slow back down. The act of calming Sylvester's mother had kept her calm and down to earth.

"You gonna be okay?"

"Yeah, thanks Honey. I'm so happy Sylvester has you. We have to get together, you and I."

"I'd like that, too," said Annie. "Thanks for. . . letting me know."

"Bye bye Honey, keep up your prayers."

"I will."

Joan stepped off the bus and turned the opposite way from home. The snow still blanketed the sidewalk, and it was a crunchy kind of snow, not so easily slipped on. Shoppers clustered in twos and threes dotted the wide sidewalks and parking areas. This was ordinarily her most favorite time of the year. It was something so wondrous and merry, with the streets gay and full of life. It was hard to mix into it the sudden sobering uncertainty of things.

Annie rarely called her at work so when Joan heard her voice, she knew it had to be news about Sylvester. It had left Joan stirred up and anxious. What did it actually mean, Missing in Action? They couldn't find him? He was in another camp or something? Or was he actually on a secret mission and nobody knew what had become of him?

Annie had almost laughed when Joan had suggested that. No, Annie had said, he didn't do missions, so to speak. He was just a translator. He must have been driving somewhere or maybe where he was working was hit or something. Joan wondered about that. If a place had been bombed, wouldn't they be able to identify everyone who was killed or injured?

Luckily, she had caught herself before she said what she was thinking. Who knew? Maybe Annie had thought the same thing but had put it out of her mind. In any case, Missing in Action had an ugly, frightening ring to it, and Joan was seeking the greatest best solution to calm those fears.

She arrived at her destination and knocked on the door. Ordinarily, she was intimidated by these places. She wondered about that. Why was she so shy around clergy? She guessed it was because they dressed differently and they all seemed to live in distant mysterious domiciles. The nuns from the academy led quiet, nearly cloistered lives inside a brick convent with high, stained glass windows. It was a beautiful building on the outside, and looked just like a smaller version of the church. Joan had never been inside and wondered if it looked just like the church but with a few beds instead of pews. And if that were the case, what could it possibly look like in a *priest's* house? Did their beds have blankets that looked like vestments? Did they sleep in their cleric's clothing?

The door started to open. She stood up straight and tall as if awaiting inspection.

"Why Joan Foster!" Father Bertrand said smiling. "How nice to see you. Come on in out of the cold. I

was just making a cup of tea before heading over to
the church. Will you join me?"

Joan brightened, surprised by the familiar and
enthusiastic greeting. "No thank you," she said as she
stepped over the threshold. "I've just come from
work so I've got to be going soon, Father."

"Oh, of course. Would you like to sit down?"
Father Bertrand pulled another chair beside the one
already in the little vestibule.

"Sure," said Joan, and sat down.

"So how are things with you and your lovely
parents?" Father asked.

"My parents are just fine," Joan said, "and I am,
too, actually. I just came to talk to you about or ask
about Annie."

"Annie?"

"Annie diRosa. She and I share Mom and Dad's
rental house."

"Oh yes, of course. The dear girl who runs the gift
shop."

"Father, she's just gotten terrible news."

Father's face instantly reflected sincere concern.

"Her fiancé is missing in action."

"Oh I'm so sorry."

"Yes, and they are so very close. I don't know
what to do for her."

"I am certain that you will do all you can as the
days go on," Father said. "And your prayers and
extra care for your friend will carry her further than
you can imagine. But I will say I only recently
received a call about this very same thing from

another woman, regarding her husband. St. Benedict's is very hard hit this week. I will tell you that in addition, I have had bad news about a dear friend of mine."

"Oh I'm so sorry!" said Joan.

He smiled. "Thank you, Joan," he said. "I have been thinking about this since I got the news this morning. Sometimes the best way to grow in strength is to gather in numbers. We gain a perspective on our pain by knowing about others' trials or maybe just knowing that there are others sharing oh, grief or fear, or even confusion, or doubts. These times are a challenge to our well-being, both spiritual and emotional, too. And where do we go in times of challenge?" Father smiled warmly. "We go to God of course."

Joan smiled. She felt a sudden sense of peace, as if everything would be all right. She took a deep breath and let it out.

"Thank you, Father," she said.

"And I want to thank *you* for bringing this to me. I think maybe a special Mass would be the right thing, dedicated to the safe passage of our loved ones and their speedy return. I don't know if we could get the word out fast enough, but I would like to invite the whole parish, and have the Mass tomorrow, so we don't run too close to the Christmas Eve and Midnight Mass."

Joan nodded smiling. "It'll be such a boost to everyone's morale."

Just then, Celeste bounced around the corner and popped right up onto Father's lap. "Speaking of morale," he said, "this little gal has brought quite a bit of Christmas joy to an old scarecrow like me."

"Oh, isn't she sweet!" said Joan, petting the little animal. "I didn't know you had a cat."

"Either did I," Father Bertrand said laughing.

Walking home, Joan felt back on track. Her heart was filled once again with hope and she was eager to share it with Annie.

As Father closed the door, he was struck again by the thought of how evil utterly fails in the face of good.

Chapter Seventeen

"You saw *what*?" Pauline called across to Rose as they walked awkwardly down the sidewalk. Pauline and Clara kept up a punishing pace, while Rose, between them, had to run a few steps every so often to keep up.

"I tell you, I saw that young girl, Joan, coming right out of the rectory yesterday afternoon. And I *know* what I saw," Rose puffed.

"You saw a parishioner exiting the rectory," said Clara.

"I want to know what she saw," Pauline said.

"She told you what she saw!"

"I saw her," said Rose. "She was coming down the steps, all dressed up, too, looking like she was dressed for an important meeting—or a *date*."

"That's because she was on her way home from work!" called Bernice from behind, trying to catch up. "She was stopping in to see Father after work. She's the whole reason we got this Mass, for crying out loud!"

"Oh," said Rose, slow down. "Well. I didn't know."

Bernice stifled the temptation to say *you didn't want to know!* She contented herself with an audible sigh and exchanged glances with her grandmother.

"That'll teach you, Rose Parlavita," said Clara.

"Well, I still don't think it's well advised," said Rose.

The Mass was at 11:00 a.m. The choir was to sing.
Bernice wrestled her way through the crowd at the
front doors, thinking sometimes it pays to be short.
An older woman gave her a sharp look as Bernice
stumbled, and steadied herself by grabbing the
woman's purse.

"I was just. . ."

The woman raised her eyebrows and turned to
walk the other way, her hand protectively around her
bag.

Bernice felt herself beginning to perspire. It's not
that big of a deal, she told herself. Calm down!

She heard the opening chords to one of the
hymns as Bitsy provided beautiful meditative music.
Of the people attending, more than half had either
family overseas in the War or were mourning the loss
of a loved one.

Candles had been lit and placed on side tables out
of respect for the dead, each candle representing
someone lost during the past year. Another table held
many more candles, each tied at the base with a
yellow ribbon, representing a loved one in harm's
way. The presence of the candles, their gentle,
constant flames, and comforting glow, reminded her
of her times in Philly. That very morning, she had
spent considerable time on the telephone getting
advice and asking for special prayers.

"You look nice today," said Carol as Bernice
entered the choir loft.

"Thank you!" Bernice said, a little out of breath. "Boy, those stairs give a kid a workout!"

Carol smiled and sat down.

"Listen," said Bernice. "I've been meaning to have a chat with you."

Bitsy's head popped around in their direction. My gosh, thought Bernice. She's got radar!

"Bernice, if it's about that old solo, forget it," Carol said.

Bernice was startled. "You knew what I was thinking?"

"Yeah, pretty much. And I don't really care. I've done it a bunch of times. You might say I'm pretty sick of it."

"You *might*," said Bernice. "Yeah, *you* might say that. But I wouldn't."

Carol turned to face her, a glint of ill-concealed hope on her face.

"Sure you're sick of it," giggled Bernice.

Bitsy hawked in on their conversation, one eyebrow up, head cocked, straining to hear.

"Oh my gosh, lower your voice," Bernice nearly whispered, smiling at Bitsy. When Bitsy looked the other way to turn a page, Bernice seized the opportunity. "You still want to do it!"

Carol opened her mouth to protest but nothing came out.

"Look, I have all kinds of opportunities to sing," said Bernice. "I may be doing a lot of singing in the near future. This choir is great, but the solo, Carol, that's yours. And in case you clown around and pretend you don't want it, just be sure you know what you're doing, because I have already told Bitsy I'm not doing it."

"You have?" Carol was shocked.

"Yeah, but she didn't believe me. As you can tell by her expression over there." She indicated Bitsy who was back on track with her distant investigation. "Just smile and nod," said Bernice. "Smile and nod."

Carol giggled. "That's Bitsy."

"In fact," Bernice lowered her voice, "I'm not even going to be here Midnight Mass. I'm planning to sit with my friends and family." She pointed down. "Down there."

At last Carol's face brightened. "Really?" she said cautiously.

"Aha! I knew it!" said Bernice, giggling. "I knew it!"

"Shh!" Bitsy hissed frantically. "We're starting."

"Hey, Bob," Dick said, "What do you make of this?"

"What's that?"

"Listen, let me read this to you: 'I don't know very much about the workings of the military, but it sounds as if you have everything in your watch well in hand. I trust that whatever decisions you make will be the right ones.' This is part of a letter, from Joan."

Bob leaned across the narrow space that separated their two bunks. "What's she talking about?"

"I don't know. It sounds like she's, you know, trying to be formal or something. It doesn't sound anything like her friendly letters from before. You think she's met someone else and changed her mind about me?"

"Oh gee, Dick, I really don't know. But I told you before, the gals want to know where they stand. You kept her dangling. I hope that wasn't a big mistake for you, buddy."

Dick furrowed his brow. "I did?"

"Hell yeah! Did you propose?"

"Well no, but I thought it was understood—"

"Understood nothing. Girls aren't like the military—they don't follow a regimen. How is she supposed to know you want to marry her? She probably thinks exactly the opposite. I told you, man."

Dick was getting irritated. "Okay, you told me, but I thought I had the situation well in hand—" He stopped dead in his tracks. "That's what the letter said, isn't it?"

"Aw, she's not that. . . smart. . . is she? Is she trying to. . . What's she doing?" Bob finished.

"You're asking *me?*"

Bob took the letter and read it aloud. "'I don't know very much about the workings of the military, but it sounds as if you have everything in your watch well in hand. I trust that whatever decisions you make will be the right ones.'   Maybe, you know, it's a hint or something. Okay, she says, Whatever decisions you make will be the right ones. Decisions. You get it?"

Dick stared at Bob. "Well . . . "

Bob put down the letter and clapped a hand on Dick's shoulder. "Okay. I think what she's saying, and boy you've caught yourself a live one, is that she hopes or thinks you're considering a *decision*. Or possibly, and boy, I hope this isn't it, *she's* got a decision to make."

"You mean somebody else, some other fellow might have—"

"Well that I don't know, but maybe she's just sitting and thinking, hmm, do I want to go on with this or should I just start looking—"

"But why," Dick said, becoming agitated, "would she look around when she and I. . . Oh, I think I see what you mean."

Bob stood back and appraised Dick. He was the highest merit award winner for bravery and he was brilliant on the gunnery field. But when it came to women, well, his headlights sure did go dim.

The two sat there in a silence for a while until someone down the hallway flicked on the radio. In the Mood blasted out into the stark hallway, echoing through like an explosion of goodwill.

Dick stood up, his eyes intense, knuckles white grasping the letter. "How do I get in the queue for long distance calls?"

"Okay," Bob said, breaking into a grin, "Now you're talking, buddy!"

Later that night, Bob sat at his desk. "I think we've finally got Dick on the right path," he wrote to Laureen. "Boy! You scheming females! Hitler won't have a chance if they ever put you gals in charge of strategy and maneuvers."

Chapter Eighteen

"How does it look in the back?"

"Oh Joanie it looks beautiful," said Annie. "Just gorgeous."

"Well this material wrinkles so easily. Do you think when I sit down it will crinkle up and then look terrible when I stand up again?"

Helen stood in the kitchen doorway, a green and white dishtowel embroidered with a Christmas tree in one hand and the pot she was drying in the other. "You'll probably have your coat on anyway, Joan."

"Oh Helen, I'm sorry!" said Joan suddenly. "We should be in there helping, not worrying about how we look. Is there anything left to do in the kitchen?"

"No, no, girls. You're only young once. You go ahead and fuss. I enjoy working in my kitchen, especially around the holidays."

Annie sighed, entering the kitchen. "Helen, I wish I had your strength."

Helen put down the towel and pot. "It's not so much strength, Honey," she said putting an arm around Annie. "I'm lucky because I know. My heart just tells me. It's not that I heard anything more or anything like that. I just believe Harry is fine. So I'm not distraught. I can celebrate this Christmas, this Midnight Mass, with the true joy it's meant to be celebrated with."

"But how do you know? How *can* you know? I think I start to feel that Sylvester's fine, just lost or without communication or something but then I start to get that feeling that an elephant is growing in my lungs—"

"Cheese Annie! That's gross!" giggled Bernice.

Annie giggled in spite of herself. "Okay, well a cornstalk maybe, just something wild and filling me up inside and I start thinking—"

"Well *there's* your problem," Bernice said. "When you have faith, you don't go thinking about all those dark possibilities. You just simply ask for the help you need, and then put your trust in God. That's the end of it. Worry and cornstalks, or elephants or whatever's making you a mess are no longer necessary."

Annie turned to Bernice, eyes wide. "You know, I think I'm finally starting to get used to you being a fountain of wisdom. I don't know where it all came from, but I'm glad it's here." She hugged Bernice. "But you're still really short."

Bernice hit her on the elbow.

Helen smiled as she returned to her work. "I think you all look fantastic," she called as the other headed for the mirror in the living room. "Annie, you're a raving beauty."

"I agree," said Joan, admiring her friend. "With your tall slim figure and gorgeous hair, you could wear a burlap sack and still look beautiful."

"Such praise! I don't think I can take it!"

"Well, I think we're all beautiful," said Bernice, "but if we want to sit in a pew and not stand at the back, we'd better get moving."

"I'm with you," Annie said smiling. But deep inside, despite Bernice's good and encouraging words, she feared what news would come in the days that followed. It was her burden though, and she was determined to carry it alone.

The rich, joyful music filled Father's heart and soul with the hope brimming over from the phone call he had received only moments before he Mass had begun. As he walked to the podium to begin his Christmas homily, he recalled the conversation.

"I wanted you to hear the news as soon as I received it," the Cardinal had said.

"News?"

"Regarding your friend, Alphonse Kuchesky," he continued. "We can no longer be sure that he was among the ones executed that awful day of the massacre. The bodies found in the shallow grave belonged to a small group of people who had just arrived at the safe house. The one local man who was brave enough to talk to the priest investigating on behalf of the Allies told him that he believed Monsignor Kuchesky and his group had no longer been there when the Nazis arrived. The man knew the Monsignor by his laugh and his generosity. It was shortly after Monsignor Kuchesky departed that this new group appeared, the ones who had been so heartlessly slaughtered. "I wanted you to know immediately," the Cardinal said, "that the fate of our Monsignor Kuchesky is now, at least, unknown. There is still hope."

Father Bertrand hung up from that conversation feeling that Divinity had intervened; it had been the love of God and His angels at work. Instantly his spirit radiated hope and the joy that came from that hope, so similar to that which the shepherds and Wise Men felt on that very first Christmas. His eyes sparkled as he relayed his Christmas message, encouraging the strength and endurance so evident in his congregation and ending with his heartfelt gratitude for the love and generosity, and sincere prayers offered on the behalf of all that so many had shown through the continuing and very difficult times. "As long as we persevere with God in our hearts, we will make it through these painful times. Maybe we won't be the same as when we started, but we will grow strong in the Kingdom of God. Have a Merry Christmas, everyone!"

Helen's eyes shone as they walked through the streets. "All right," she said, "everyone home to my house for a nice Christmas punch!"

They had walked to St. Benedict's, hoping to see falling snow on the way home. But while it was quiet and blackout dark, the snow was not falling.

Rose, Pauline, and their sodality friends Maudie and Lois also walked. "Did she say to come to her house?" Rose asked.

"Oh she wasn't talking to us, Silly," answered Pauline. "We're all coming over my house, don't you remember? Where's Mother?"

"Here I am," Clara said, pushing between Maudie and Lois. "I'm coming."

"Oh, yes, yes. Now I remember. You're right," said Rose.

The bells rang behind them, oblivious to the dark, sending parishioners home with Christmas joy in their hearts.

"What are you plans for tomorrow?" Annie asked Bernice, as they took off their coats in Helen's hallway.

"I don't know for sure," she started to say when Helen cut in.

"You're all invited here for Christmas dinner of course!" she said. "This is an opportunity I wouldn't miss!"

"But my mom—" began Bernice.

"She's invited, too, and yours and yours," she said to Annie and Joan. "Everyone's invited!"

"Oh, Annie," Joan said, "Mom has invited your family to our house."

"No kidding, Joanie," Annie said smiling. "That's so kind of them. I will let them know. I don't think Mom was planning anything big with Paulie away and all. But I know she won't come unless she can bring something, like cheesecake or pastries or something."

"I don't think she'll have to fight too hard for that privilege!" Joan laughed.

"So. . . " Bernice said, "is it just your *parents* that concern themselves with good manners, or are you planning to. . ."

Joan and Helen laughed. "Yeah," said Annie sharply, "I *think* I can remember my manners— Cheesie Pete, Bernice!"

"What flavor manners will you remember, Annie?" Helen asked.

"Whatever flavor—hey, how about cherry pie?"

"I was thinking in terms of that cheesecake," said Bernice.

"Oh you were, were you? You were already thinking in terms of something?" Annie smirked.

"I like the sound of the cherry pie," said Helen.

"Does your bakery make anything chocolate?" Joan asked.

Annie's eyes bugged out in mock astonishment, "Well for heavens' sakes! Why don't I just bring the whole bakery!"

"I think that's an excellent idea," said Helen, pouring the tea. "But in the meantime, let's enjoy some nice hot tea and chat. It was sure a cold walk home!"

After they were seated and sipping Helen's delicious spicy tea, Bernice stood up and cleared her throat.

"Are you going to make a speech?" Annie said.

"Yes, I am," said Bernice in a calm but happy voice.

Something in her voice made the girls look up. Helen smiled, looking down at her cup.

"Bernice?" Joan started.

"Nothing bad," she said. "I just want Helen to know and Annie to know, that the Sisters of St. Benedict of Philadelphia, the whole convent, is remembering our very specific intentions tonight at their Midnight Mass for the safe deliverance from harm and return home of Harry and Sylvester."

Annie's mouth opened but nothing came out. She looked at Joan who was equally dumfounded. Finally Annie said, "Helen?"

Helen sat smiling up at Bernice. "Bernice, that's a wonderful thing you've done. Thank you so much!"

"Yes!" Annie said, "how very kind of you and—I don't know what to say. I would never have thought to have those angels of mercy intercede in prayer. You are just wonderful, Bernice!" Annie stood up to give her a hug.

"I'm so glad we could be together tonight, the four of us," said Bernice. "Because that isn't all I have to tell you."

Annie sat down again. "What?" she said apprehensively.

Joan grabbed Annie's hand. "Yeah, what?"

"I think this is the perfect time to announce or whatever the right word is, that with God's grace, and my perseverance, I will be joining the Sisters of St. Benedict as a postulant, with the hope of making myself conspicuous for life," she smiled, "in the habit of a fully avowed Benedictine Sister."

Annie and Joan gasped in unison, looked at each other, then back at Bernice. Joan was the first to speak. "Bernice! Oh my gosh! Bernice!"

Annie grabbed her in a bear hug and then opened her arms to Helen and Joan who joined in. Annie's eyes were wet with tears as she drew back to see Bernice's face. "I am so, I just," but she fell short of a complete sentence.

Bernice smiled and squeezed her hand.

"Thank God," said Helen. "I am so grateful for you, for all of you, for this wonderful night, everything."

Joan looked at Helen. "I am too," she said. "But you know, Helen, somehow I don't think this has come as a surprise to you."

Helen smiled and looked at Bernice.

"Yeah Helen," said Annie, "you got an inside track or something?"

"Yeah, she's got an in with the nuns in Philly," said Bernice laughing. "No! I talked to Helen. She's very comforting. It's been a difficult decision, but she was there for me, and she was kind enough to keep my secret until I was ready to share it."

"Oh," said Joan.

"Oh don't pout, Joanie!" said Bernice.

"No, no, I'm not pouting."

Annie and Helen exchanged glances. "Well I for one am very excited for you," said Annie, "but I don't mind saying I will sure miss you."

"Ditto," said Bernice. "Who you gonna to kick around now anyway? Joan, you better watch your step!" Everyone laughed, Joan joining in weakly.

"Let's sit down and have our tea before it's iced tea," said Helen. "And some of our Christmas treats!"

After their impromptu Christmas Eve party ended, having included rounds of O Come All Ye Faithful and Away in a Manger, Bernice went home to Pauline, and Annie and Joan walked looking at the sky, hoping for just a few flakes of snow.

"I don't think we'll see any snow tonight," Annie said. "But even despite that, and despite my news about Sylvester, I feel full of hope and bursting with Christmas spirit."

"Now that's happy news!"

"I don't know if I ever really told you how much it meant to me that you arranged that special Mass. It really touched my heart. I think of how I would be without you, and I get sick thinking how desolate this all would be."

Joan turned, wide-eyed. "Annie, I don't know what to say. I guess you know I feel the same. I've been really down since, well, you know. Dick doesn't seem to want to move toward marriage. But your sense of humor and your pseudo wisecracking upbeat attitude just always lifts me up."

"Well, you know I'll do whatever I can. But I think you're giving up too easily. I think you've taken up residence in his heart for a permanent stay. He's just, you know. . . slow."

Joan giggled in spite of herself. "I'll tell him you said that."

Annie shrugged. "Okay with me. It's true enough!"

They both giggled.

"Isn't Bernice something?" Joan asked after a few moments. "If she had told me that news about herself even 3 months ago, I would have said you are joking. There is no possible way you could be serious. But even still, it was a shock."

"It was. But a good one. Oh gosh we'll miss her!" Annie's voice cracked.

Joan put her arm around her. "Me, too."

They walked down the quiet lane, no moon or stars, yet somewhere up high, little tiny crystals were forming, and just as they turned up their walk, the first snowflakes of Christmas began to fall.

Chapter Nineteen

Helen lit a candle. It sat securely in a deep votive candle holder, but its light filled the room. "Sweet Jesus," she whispered. "Thank you." Then she blew out the candle and fell excitedly into bed like a school girl.

"Are you sure, ma?" Annie said. "I can drive you. The snow's not that deep."

Joan looked out the window. She wore her cozy bathrobe and holey bed socks that she'd had since 6th grade. She looked over at Annie, also still dressed in PJs. A telephone sure was a luxury, she thought. She felt sorry for the people who didn't have one. Especially on Christmas. Annie's voice cut into her thoughts before they could go further.

"All right," Annie went on. "But I gotta come ovah anyway, to get the desserts. . . yeah. I'm taking a cheesecake and one of them pies. . . Cherry, if it's all right." She caught Joan's eye. "Oh! And a slice of chocolate cake, if that's all right. . . no, not the whole thing . . . no—"

Joan giggled.

"Okay, I'm sure we could find a place for it. As long as you got enough," Annie continued. "I'll be ovah in a little while."

"They can't make it," Joan said as Annie hanged up the phone.

"Right. But they want me to take some stuff."

"Your manners?"

They laughed.

"Yeah," Annie said. "I got all three flavored manners."

"Oh yum!" said Joan. "Mom and Dad aren't coming either, though. They have a lot of food and I think some of our relatives and coming, Margie and Eddy, and the cousins and all. I didn't think they were doing anything, but they must have made last minute plans. I'm going over in a minute, to spend some time with them today."

"Yeah, me, too," said Annie. "I'll race you to the bathroom!"

"Did she invite Rose?" Pauline whispered to Clara as Rose lagged behind.

"No," Clara said. "Rose invited herself."

Pauline sighed and shook her head.

"I hope she's made a nice dinner!" Rose called. "I'd hate to walk all this way for just franks and beans."

Helen opened the curtains. It had snowed at least 3 inches overnight. There had been very little wind and the delicate white flakes clung to the branches of her sweet gum and maple trees creating a dreamlike scene. She turned back to the stove.

"It's gorgeous, isn't it?" Joan said, drying and placing the silverware.

"It truly is," said Helen. "I was thinking we weren't going to get any snow."

"Me, too. I'm glad it came."

"There's something very cozy and sweet about snow on Christmas, even if you have to travel in it—which I don't!" Helen laughed.

"How many plates, Helen?" Bernice called from the dining room.

"We're an even eight," Helen answered. "Father's coming, and your mom and grandma, of course, and then Rose, too."

"Oh I didn't know you asked her," Bernice said, setting the plates around the table. "My, these are beautiful." She stood back to admire the English bone china labeled St. Michael. It had lacey silver feathers around the edges of the plate, with small royal blue baskets of flowers in varying rich shades and light grey swords, which stood crossed in the very center, exquisitely outlined in platinum. The matching cups and saucers had pink and silver feathers around the edges with a brilliant blue flower edged in silver, which sat in the center of each cup and saucer.

"Thank you," Helen said. "When we picked those out, Harry said. . ."

The girls exchanged glances.

"Go on, Helen," Joan said gently.

"I'm okay," Helen said. "I'm remembering. Harry said we'd better find a pattern that had something manly in it or he wasn't going to be a party to it." She chuckled. "With this pattern, I think we're both pretty well represented."

"Yep," said Joan. "Together."

"Okay, okay," said Bernice. "Where's the dessert, that's what I want to know."

"Well, we've still got time," Helen said. "Joan, go ahead and put out the cheese and celery and we'll have some wine tonight, too, if anybody's interested."

"You never told us what you have in the oven," Joan said.

"I didn't?"

"No. Can I look?"

"Oh, I guess so," said Helen.

The three of them crowded around the oven and peeked through the door as Helen opened it. Joan and Bernice gasped.

"How in the world—"

"*Where* in the world did you get that?" Bernice finished.

Inside stood a prime rib roast, fully five and one-half pounds, surrounded by potatoes, and little carrots that glistened with a glaze that promised to be both sweet and spicy. The roast was nearly done, the outer edges tucked under the bones looking crisp and delicious.

"Oh, I have my ways!" Helen said with a twinkle in her eye.

The two girls sighed in delight, dreaming of a slice of the rare and cherished extravagance.

"Working the black market, eh?" Annie said laughing as she entered the kitchen.

"Merry Christmas, Annie!" said Joan. "Were the roads bad?"

"Well, I had to drive very slowly, but it's okay. I'm just glad I'm near home! What's that great beast in the oven? You got friends in high places, Helen?"

"I don't, but Father Bertrand has," Helen said smiling. "A parishioner brought this to the rectory and he, knowing he'd be with us today, brought it over a couple of days ago. I thought it would make a nice surprise."

"It sure did," said Bernice. "What a marvelous surprise."

"Mom and Dad will be sad they missed it!" Joan said. "But they had their chance."

"Oh let's hear some music," said Annie. "Do you have your record player warmed up, Helen?"

"It's not working," Helen said closing the oven door. "But we've got the radio."

As Annie brought in her desserts, Bernice tuned in the radio, and Joan helped Helen in the kitchen. By 4:00, the curtains and shades were drawn, and everyone had arrived.

"Let's turn down the music while Father says grace," said Helen. "We can turn it up afterwards."

Father Bertrand smiled. "What a warm group to celebrate Christmas with. Thanks again for inviting me, Mrs. Ashenbach."

"Of course! We were so happy you could come!" Helen said. For a moment Helen felt awkward, the pronoun "we" not quite fitting her current circumstance, but she felt certain Father didn't think she was being pretentious. She started to thank him again for the roast when suddenly a solid and very disconcerting knock sounded on the door. It was a crisp knock, exactly three times, done in militaristic rhythmic precision. Helen's eyes grew wide. She looked around the table. Bernice had frozen on her way back to the table. Annie and Joan looked at each other and then slowly at Helen. It couldn't be. Nobody would bring such news on Christmas Day.

Then a second time came the knock-knock-knock startling Helen again as if it were the first time. She got up, using the table to steady herself, and slowly made her way toward the door. Bernice took hold of one arm and Annie and Joan crowded in next to her at the other. They allowed her a little more room as she walked the final few steps to the door, around a slight corner and out of view from those still seated at the table. Helen approached the door and peered through the peep hole. She saw green and her heart pounded. "It's green," she whispered, turning only slightly toward the girls, her mouth suddenly as dry as a baked potato. "I can't see anything but Army green." She lowered her head, and opened the door, looking as if she were preparing to receive a knock on the head.

Once the door was opened, she slowly raised her head, wondering on the way up why she had not heard the traditional, "Mrs. Ashenback?" She looked up, expecting to see a grim-faced major, hat tucked in between his arm and side, holding a folded flag. Instead she saw a bandaged soldier, strong and steady, smiling, dropping his duffle bag and holding his arms open wide.

"Sorry, Honey," he said, "I forgot my key!"

"Harry!" Helen shrieked. "Harry!"

As Harry enfolded her into his arms, Bernice, Joan, and Annie rushed forward like 3 little girls on Christmas morning, shrieking and giggling nervously.

"Oh my gosh!" said Joan, tears clouding her vision instantly. Then she drew back. "Let's give them a little privacy."

"I don't think so!" Annie called out, "Harry! You made it back!" She grabbed a piece of his arm and Bernice snuck in between Helen and him. Joan shook her head, rushing forward to embrace them all.

"What a godsend," Helen said, trying to stop sobbing. "I've missed you so."

"We've all missed you," Joan said. "Helen's been so good to us and she's held out faith the whole time, but we were so worried. Oh thank God you made it back!"

"Yeah, Honey," Harry said turning to Helen, "I guess we took the long way around." He laughed.

"Well as long as you made it!" Helen cried, burying her head in his chest. And then pulling back suddenly. "And what timing!"

"Yeah, special delivery for Christmas Dinner," Bernice said. "I call that pretty good timing."

"I want to hear everything, everything," Annie said, "but guys, let's get him in out of the cold!"

"Yes, Harry, come on in—" Helen began, taking his arm.

But Harry put up a hand. "No, wait," he said. "I'm so sorry to do this to you Honey, and girls, as I'm sure you've put a lot of time into whatever that heavenly smell is coming from the kitchen, but I've got a lonesome soldier from my unit here on leave, and he's got nowhere to go for Christmas. Would we be able to scrape together another plateful?"

"Oh Harry, you don't even have to ask," said Helen, giving him a squeeze back and peering around the corner. "Oh there he is! Don't be so shy, soldier, you're welcome, come on in out of the cold!"

"My gosh, yes, don't let the poor man stand out there in the snow!" Annie said.

The soldier had stood shyly, his back to the door and a few steps away. The girls were curious and craned their necks to see what this poor forlorn soldier looked like. As he turned to face them, both he and Harry began to laugh.

"Sylvester!" Annie screamed. Chairs being pushed back from the table could be heard, followed by a little herd of curiosity approaching the door.

"Oh Harry!" said Helen again. "Sylvester!"

"Well why don't yous all get inside," Bernice said flatly, "before everybody gets pneumonia?"

Joan laughed, tears streaming down her face. Annie and Sylvester embraced, instantly in a world of their own, snowflakes twinkling onto Annie's long dark hair and melting on her face. Joan gave her a nudge.

"Annie," she giggled. "Come on you guys. The teacher's watching."

"You got that right. No fraternizing."

Sylvester and Annie took a breath for the first time since they'd caught sight of each other and together moved toward to open door, as if they were dancing in promenade.

"I feel like I'm in dream," Annie whispered.

"I'm looking at a dream," Sylvester whispered back. "I knew I'd find you here."

Annie smiled and shook her head slowly back and forth.

As the men hung their snowy clothes near the radiators per Helen's instructions, Joan and Bernice exchanged smiles.

"I can't believe it!" Joan whispered to her.

"And yet, it's happening," said Bernice. "Just like the miracles we all prayed for."

Annie joined them and they clumped together like a football huddle. "I can hardly talk," Annie said. "I just am so happy."

Once two additional chairs were joyfully added to the table, Father Bertrand said the grace, and passed around the food. Despite the butterflies in his stomach, Sylvester had no trouble ploughing in the magnificent feast. Harry scarcely came up for air.

"Well, Harry, don't keep us in suspense," Rose said. "How in the world did you make it back? I heard you were missing. And what circumstances led you to find Annie's young man alone at Christmas?"

Bernice giggled. "I think the second part was just a joke, Mrs. Parlavita."

"Oh."

"I was assigned to Cap—Sergeant Ashenback," said Sylvester. "Oh gosh, this is good!" He paused to take another bite of his slice of prime rib. "I know you all are getting short-shrifted because of me, and I want you to know I sure appreciate it!"

Everyone laughed.

"But were you assigned to Harry's unit?" Rose persisted.

"Yes, he was from the start," Harry cut in. "But we had no idea we were 'related' until we happened to be talking a long time later. And we were trying to find Bobby, and—"

"Who's Bobby?" asked Annie, suddenly breaking from her love trance.

Sylvester tried to stay above the shadow of sorrow and it passed quickly as Harry continued explaining what had happened. At the disclosure of the explosion, Annie gripped Sylvester's hand tightly. "You could have been killed," she whispered as Harry continued.

"I couldn't possibly be!" Sylvester whispered back, smiling at her. "There were so many brave men there," he said. "Not all American. In fact, I was actually saved by an Italian merchant shipman named Rico. The poor fellow only regained consciousness a couple days before we left."

"Saved by a gumbah," Bernice giggled.

"God bless that man," said Father.

"Pass the rolls," said Pauline.

"He was injured himself, but somehow, I still don't know how, we got off that ship, past the flames, and picked up by the Americans in the harbor. The nuns took care of me and put me back together. It was a really, it was just a miraculous and holy experience," he finished, his eyes clouding. "Nothing like Harry's, though."

"Harry's?" Helen looked up sharply. "What do you mean?"

Just then, the phone rang.

"That'll be the newspapers," Bernice said.

"You clown," Helen laughed. "I'll be right back. Have some of the casserole honey, there's plenty. And I want to hear what Sylvester's talking about."

Seconds later, Helen called from the kitchen. "Joan, Joanie honey, there's a phone call for you!"

"Is it Mom?" Joan asked, leaving the table. "I wonder if they want to come over for dessert."

"It's a very special call, so don't waste your time dawdling."

As Joan hurried in, Helen jammed the phone into her hand, she said, "I'll give *you* some privacy now!" She giggled and hurried back to the dining room.

"Hello?" Joan said, still expecting it to be her mother.

"Well hello there from across the miles," Dick said. He hit himself on the forehead, thinking what am I, a radio announcer or something?

But Joan was ecstatic. "Dick! What a surprise! Well. . . Merry Christmas!"

"Yes, uh that's right, Merry Christmas! I was extremely lucky to get this second call—"

"Oh, you tried before?"

"Well, yes, but at a different house, or at your house, I mean. And normally you only get one try but since it was Christmas and since, well I had a special call to make—"

"I'm so glad you got to. I've missed you," said Joan, breathless. "It's hard to hear you, Dick. There's a lot of static on the line. It must be because we're so far apart."

"Can you hear me okay now?" he asked loudly.

"Yes, that's better. How are you?"

"Oh, doggonnit, I'm pretty nervous," he said, "and I think we've only got about 45 more seconds."

"Oh gosh. Nervous talking to me? It hasn't been that long," Joan said. "I'm the same old Joan."

"No nervous because I need to say something, well, ask something, and boy oh boy I don't like using the telephone, but I think it's best I do since we won't see each other for a while."

"You want to test something, Dick? Is that what you said?"

"No, I have a question, a question."

"I'm sorry, it sounded like you said I'm a Texan, Texan." Joan was trying her absolute best to understand him, but the noise on the line was growing more overwhelming.

Oh brother, thought Dick. Whatever made me think this was going to work? Let me try one more time. "Joanie," he said.

"Yes, Dick?"

"Will. . . you. . . marry. . . me? Will you marry me?"

Joan was dumbfounded. "Did you ask me to marry you?"

The door to the kitchen moved inward, and three sets of eyes appeared at the door frame. Joan turned away from them, her heart aglow and butterflies lifting her from the inside.

"Yes!" Dick said as loudly as he could. The guys behind him in line were in full guffaw mode. "I'll make this up to you," he growled at them under his breath, having no effect on the level of their mirth.

"Well then," Joan said, "yes!"

"Yes! It's a yes!" shouted Helen, Bernice, and Annie, cheering.

"Shh!" Joanie said laughing and listening hard into the phone.

"I only have 5 seconds left," Dick said, "but I love you, Joan. Thank you, I'll write soon, I'll write tonight, I'll write right now."

"Oh, me too!" Joan said, "And I love you too!"

"Have a wonderful Christmas, too and—"

"I'm sorry," the operator said flatly. "Your three minutes are up. This telephone call will terminate." And with that, they were disconnected.

Joan looked at the phone. "I'm pretty sure I heard that. Did you hear that?" she asked, looking at the girls.

"We heard," Helen said, embracing her. "What a marvelous day!"

"Oh Annie, Bernice, is it true?"

"Well you heard *him*," Annie laughed. "We only heard *you*."

"Of course, it's true," said Bernice. "Of course, it is!"

"Harry," called Helen merrily, "Have a cigar!"

"Him, too?" said Harry, jumping to his feet. "How 'bout a stogie, Sly?"

"I'm not done eating, but I'll hold it for later," said Sly.

"So *he* is Sly!" exclaimed Helen, catching Annie's eye. "I should have known!"

"Those old smelly things?" Clara said, "In the house?"

"Whatever Harry wants," Helen said embracing her long-lost husband. Quietly, she said to him, "I never lost faith. I knew you would be all right."

"I had faith in you, and I knew you'd hang in there," Harry whispered back. "St. Joseph was with me." He patted his wallet pocket.

"Hey, no funny stuff in front of the kids," Bernice said.

"See that? She's practicing already," Annie teased.

"I got my eye on you two, also," Bernice laughed.

From across the room, Helen said, "So *that's* why we got the Missing notification?"

"Yes," Harry explained. "The military is very delayed in those notifications. By the time you got them, we were probably no longer missing. Ironically, we both got leave because of our injuries."

As Harry and Sylvester regaled stories of their survival to Pauline, Clara, and Father Bertrand, Rose drifted off sitting upright in her chair. The girls, their hearts filled to the brim, cleared the dishes, listening. Helen caught sight of the Irish cup, mysteriously mended, no longer chipped, hanging as always on its assigned hook in the hutch. She looked around the room for any suspicious response to her having sighted it. Everyone was absorbed in other matters. Helen smiled and shook her head slightly, as she carried a tray into the kitchen.

The winter sun set on Abbotsville in its rich tradition and joyous celebration of the birth of Christ. With the wealth of happiness secure in their hearts that that glorious day had brought, the girls felt the glow of the knowledge that miracles were still around, and sometimes granted to those who serve.

The End.

Thank you for reading
The Call to Serve!

I sincerely hope you enjoyed it!
See what else I have by looking at my website,
www.CeceWhittakerStories.com.

I would love to hear from you!

Sincerely,
Cece Whittaker

Made in the USA
Middletown, DE
14 March 2020